I pressed my face against the glass. There w~~
something between the stage and the big hall, so~~
sort of huge, dark grid, or frame. Some sort of *barrier*.

I was trying to work out what the thing might be,
when I saw the figure. On the stage it stood, behind
the barrier. I don't know why I hadn't noticed it
before. Dressed all in white it was, with white
sticking-up hair, standing as if the whole stage, indeed
the whole Guildhall, belonged to him, or her, or it.
With firmly-planted legs, and crossed arms, it stared
directly down the hall – *at me*.

The air felt thick suddenly. Thick and still. The hair
rippled on the back of my head. I turned and f~~
struggling through the frozen garden on lumpen ~~
and tumbling into the stream bed. Had I seen ~
Christmas angel, I asked myself, or had it be~~
ghost? A lifetime of Grandpa's stories had ha~~
prepared me for anything. I hated myself because ~
I'd been a different sort of girl, I'd have waited to f~~
out.

But I was *me*. Just cowardly me. All I could think
about was getting home. I scrambled over our fence,
tore my coat, sped for the safety of the back door.

TYGER POOL

Pauline Fisk

RED FOX

A Red Fox Book

Published by Random House Children's Books
20 Vauxhall Bridge Road, London SW1V 2SA

A division of Random House UK Ltd
London Melbourne Sydney Auckland
Johannesburg and agencies throughout the world

5 7 9 10 8 6 4

First published by The Bodley Head Children's Books 1994

Red Fox edition 1996

Printed and bound in Great Britain by
Cox & Wyman Ltd, Reading, Berkshire

Papers used by Random House UK Limited
are natural, recyclable products made from wood grown in
sustainable forests. The manufacturing processes conform to
the environmental regulations of the country of origin

RANDOM HOUSE UK Limited Reg. No. 954009

ISBN 0 09 926411 0

CONTENTS

for the roses

PART ONE

THE ROCKETS

1

There are boarded-up houses down Planetree Avenue, these days. It's hard to believe how fast things are changing. Of course, Viola remains at the Old Guildhall, but it seems so long now since she moved there, so long since our first meeting, down in Whiteley Wood. It might have been a whole lifetime ago.

There was a time – not so long ago – when we wouldn't have gone down to Whiteley Wood for anything. But life goes on. We have a job to do – a duty to perform, you might even say. So, down among the ancient trees we venture again, and there's graffiti on the War Memorial and the paths have become a racing track for mountain bikes. But saplings have been planted to replace the trees that came down. And our friends, the swans, are back on Tyger Pool, gliding between the litter, heads held high.

Tyger Pool! Sometimes we peer beneath its surface, close as we dare, but a fine veil always hides its secrets. They lie still and deep and undisturbed beneath the watercress and hovering dragonflies.

We hardly can believe that there are *things* down there. We hardly can believe what happened.

When I was small, I wanted to be a character in one of Grandpa's stories – a dragon-slayer, or an enchanted princess who conjured jewelled birds out of the air, or a knight who found the Holy Grail. But that was before the draining of Tyger Pool. That was before Aunt Cat, and Pretty Polly, and the star-window.

Then, all I wanted was to return to those endless days when nothing ever seemed to change in our quiet bit of town. . . .

For as long as I could remember, we had lived on Planetree Avenue, with the awful Cutlers over the back in 'The Beck. B & B & Evening Meal', and quiet Miss Vine next door behind the sweeping trees of 'Forest's Glade'. Our gate said 'Habgood. Dog Patrolling. Keep Out'. But the house wasn't called Habgood – we were – and there was no dog patrolling.

The house was Grandpa's, and we had lived in it since Grandma died, when I was a baby. Grandpa ate with us, but he had his own room where he spent most of his time, making up stories, reading books and collecting newspaper cuttings for the history of his life and times, which he was compiling.

Sometimes he invited me in for cakes and tea in front of the gas fire. I loved being enclosed by his piles of books and newspapers, sunk into his leather armchair upon worn cushions which puffed out feathers every time I sat down. I loved the smell of the room – little bits of dried-up pipe tobacco, and mothbally clothes and, of course, the books. The dusty shelves full of books.

Dad used to say it was a disgrace, the way he kept that room. But Mum stuck up for him. She said he'd lived that way all his life. It was unfair to try and make him change now. We should leave him undisturbed.

And so Dad did – and we all lived undisturbed. Planetree Avenue, with its fine old trees, was in the nice bit of town. No boarded-up houses for us yet! Dustbins went out on Tuesday mornings. The milkman called to be paid on Saturdays, and the paper boy on Friday nights. It was a world that never changed – or so I thought until Mum stepped off a pavement, one crisp, autumn day when the trees were shedding their leaves and the air was heavy with nostalgia for summer. And the car that she hadn't seen, mowed her down.

Dad took me to the funeral and we stood, black crows among the autumn colours in Emmanuel's churchyard, where the graves were packed against each other like the crowds in town on Saturday afternoon. There were only Dad, and Grandpa and me, but the Cutlers made up for our lack of family. They stood on one side of us, peering in upon our misery, and the thin figure of Miss Vine in a black dress stood on the other with head turned away, and Grandpa, uncomprehending in his old age, said, 'Where's Jane?', as if he were a child again, and, 'I want my tea.'

Even after that, the world went round much as

5

it always had. Dustbins went out and the milkman and the paper boy called. Days merged into weeks. Autumn collapsed into winter. I was stunned by the spinning sameness of a world that surely should have changed because my mum had died. I went to school and came home again. Did my homework in Grandpa's room, tucked up with his books in front of the gas fire, while downstairs Dad fitted Mum's jobs frantically into his working day. He never asked me to help, but he was like that, Dad. Had to do everything himself. He organized our house so that you wouldn't know that Mum had gone. At least not by the polish on the linoleum!

At school, too, nothing changed. I was still ordinary Rosemary with the plain, brown hair. Nobody seemed to know what to say. After Miss Parker's attempts initially, nobody asked, 'Are you all right?' and I wouldn't have known how to answer if they had. My life was a dream, a dream. Beyond the houses of our road lay another row of them, and then another. I looked out at their lights at night and if I'd noticed what I was thinking, it would have been, 'How do I get out of here?'

But I didn't notice, then. I wasn't aware of anything until that day – Christmas Eve it was – when the spinning world tossed something at me which I couldn't help but see. Christmas Eve – with its routines and its rituals, whoever would have expected it to be the time for change . . .?

I remember how still everything was that afternoon, as I made my way home with my last-minute buys. Up between the quiet trees of Whiteley Wood I came. There was nobody about, and when I reached Tyger Pool not even Miss Vine was out exercizing her dog, as she often did in the afternoon.

You could hardly blame her for staying away. There had been a freezing fog for most of the day, and the air was still raw. The path round Tyger Pool was slippery with ice, and as hard as concrete. I climbed the bank at the end and came out at the bottom of our road, by the War Memorial. The distant cars passing on the main road had their headlights on already.

I was glad to arrive home. The stillness of the wood had spooked me. I was glad to hurry, two at a time up our front steps and let myself in and smell Dad's attempts at Christmas cooking.

'Is that you, Rosemary?' he called. There was nobody else who it could have been but I knew he hoped that one day, by some miracle, the clock would have turned back and I'd be Mum.

'Yes, Dad, it's me.'

I sometimes hoped for it too. I'd look at the shape of the milkman on the other side of the frosted glass and I'd think, 'It's been a mistake, and it's really *her*,' even though I could see the cap, and hear the milk bottles clinking against the crate. A mistake or a dream. . . .

'Oh well,' he said.

I hung my coat in the cupboard under the stairs, and took my bag up to my attic bedroom. Down-stairs, the hall clock struck half past three. I closed the door and leaned against it, cold as a stone, hard as the frozen path by Tyger Pool, lonely as the walk in Whiteley Wood had been. I was dreading this Christmas. But then, weren't we all?

I threw my bag of presents onto the bed, and stared at them, hating them. I couldn't face the wrapping paper in the drawer. Not yet. I'd go down to Grandpa.

No sooner had I thought it, than he tapped for me. His room was below mine. He had this way of summoning me by standing on a chair and thumping on the ceiling. 'Just a minute,' I called, covering the presents. Then, relieved to get away from them, I hurried down.

Grandpa's room was cold, because the fire wasn't lit. He was sitting at his desk, wrapped in his usual shapeless cardigan, with his thin white hair sticking up in a baby's fuzz, and his once-penetrating black eyes weakened to milky grey.

'Why don't you light the fire?' I said.

'I can't find the matches.'

I turned on the light, found the matches, and lit the hissing gas. The whole room seemed to come to life with its first pop. Grandpa, I could now see, was cutting up this morning's newspaper. I went to draw the curtains behind his bed. He began to shuffle his cuttings around, as if he didn't know what to do with them. He looked so lost.

I turned my eyes away. I couldn't bear to see him like this. I stared out of the window at the outlines of fences and garden sheds and the rows upon rows of houses, scanning them as if Father

Christmas or some miracle was out there waiting to bring purpose back to Grandpa's life.

And that was how I saw the lights at the Old Guildhall.

For as long as I could remember, the Old Guildhall had lain shuttered and empty behind our house. In living memory, it had been a silent movie cinema, post office, territorial army headquarters, theatre, village hall – even a private house. But its history stretched back beyond that for centuries. It was the oldest building in our bit of town. The Cutlers, who lived next door, complained that it brought down the value of their property. Their paying guests, they said, objected to the view. Dad, practical as ever, said that as it was empty it should be knocked down. But it was a 'listed building'. Of historical interest. So there was nothing that anyone could do.

'There's something going on at the Old Guildhall!' I said to Grandpa.

He turned in his chair, and strained to see. The arched windows of the big hall were aglow, and the porthole windows above them were as bright as full moons.

'They must be putting on a show!' he said, as if the years hadn't passed, and the Guildhall were a theatre again.

'Oh, Grandpa!' I said, and instead of feeling impatient, I envied him. Would that I could return to my yesterdays, and live in them like he did! I reached across and hugged him. His body was cold. I pulled the curtains across the window, and would have turned up the fire to the highest notch, but Dad knocked on the door. It was Christmas Eve. He wanted us to come down.

We followed him to the front room where – busy filling up his time with things he needn't have bothered with, as far as I cared – he had put up a last-minute Christmas tree. 'Come and help me,' he said, trying to sound cheerful.

I couldn't face it. I didn't want to help. I didn't want to have to smile back. I had to get out of there.

'Where are you going?' Dad said.

I grabbed my coat from under the stairs, and struggled with my boots. I would go back into town, or to buy some chips at George's Take-Away, or to investigate, yes, to investigate the lights in the Old Guildhall. . . .

Anything to get away.

'I won't be long,' I said. And I was gone.

Over the back fence I clambered, and down the bank into the stream bed which ran deep between us and the Old Guildhall. It was pitch black down there, but I didn't care. I knew this place between the fences so well – almost every overhanging branch, almost every stone beneath my boots. I caught at the root of a tree that I'd worn smooth with the times I'd swung on it, and hauled myself up high enough to peer through the Guildhall's broken fence.

There were no lights on in the building. That much I saw straight away. It must have been a trick of the frost, glittering on the windows. I must have imagined it. Oh, well. I scrambled through the fence. I'd cut through the garden to the main road and George's Take-Away. I could do with a hot bag of chips. I was freezing.

I began to cross the grass, leaving flat, white footprints behind. Beads of ice glistened on the trees above my head. I'd never seen such a bright frost before. I'd never seen the garden looking so *alive* somehow. The frost seemed almost to be creeping, like a living thing. Like stars twinkling. In the dark it was encrusting everything.

I forgot my chips, and George's Take-Away. It was the strangest thing. I could see icicles hanging like a fringe from the Guildhall's gutter, and suddenly I don't know why, but I felt as though I were floating in a sea, or in space, or in a jewelled eternity where Christmas Eve, and Christmas Day and half past three and the years of my life meant nothing any more.

I reached the Guildhall. There were patterns on the windows of such intricacy that I couldn't help but touch them. They melted instantly and I saw inside. All the shutters had been taken down. Old chairs were stacked, and curtains hung on each side of what must have been the stage. I pressed my face against the glass. There was something between the stage and the big hall, some sort of huge, dark grid, or frame. Some sort of *barrier.*

I was trying to work out what the thing might be, when I saw the figure. On the stage it stood, behind the barrier. I don't know why I hadn't noticed it before. Dressed all in white it was, with white sticking-up hair, standing as if the whole stage, indeed the whole Guildhall, belonged to him, or her, or it. With firmly-planted legs, and crossed arms, it stared directly down the hall – *at me.*

The air felt thick suddenly. Thick and still. The hair rippled on the back of my head. I turned and fled, struggling through the frozen garden on lumpen legs, and tumbling into the stream bed. Had I seen a Christmas angel, I asked myself, or had it been a ghost? A lifetime of Grandpa's stories had half-prepared me for anything. I hated myself because if I'd been a different sort of girl, I'd have waited to find out.

But I was *me.* Just cowardly me. All I could think about was getting home. I scrambled over our fence, tore my coat, sped for the safety of the back door.

And there was Dad, finishing the Christmas tree. 'It's time to do the lights,' he said, without noticing the state of me.

It had always been a special moment in our family, switching on the lights – and Mum had always done it. I turned my back on him, and drew the curtains tight, shutting out the frosty night and the thing I couldn't possibly have seen.

Dad switched on the lights, and I flung myself down in front of the telly. It was comforting, the telly was, driving all the things I didn't want to think about away.

2

Maybe I had a nightmare, maybe not. I can't remember. All I know is that I awoke sharply in the night, and Dad was standing over me saying, 'It's all right, Rosemary. Didn't mean to startle you. It's only me.'

He was holding my stocking, which I hadn't even bothered to put out – doing his Father Christmas act, even though I didn't want him to.

'I'm sorry. Did I cry out?' I said.

He should have been a sad-eyed clown, not Father Christmas. 'Go back to sleep,' was all he answered me.

I tried, but maybe I *had* woken from a bad dream. I tossed and turned. I couldn't stop imagining lights on at the Old Guildhall, and angels or ghosts penetrating my curtains with their x-ray vision, and reading the contents of my troubled mind.

Finally I crept downstairs. I wanted to bury myself deep in the dark where nobody could see me. I found some biscuits, and made myself some cocoa, which I took down into the 'utility'. It was the worst thing I could have done. I should have known better.

On rainy days, the utility had always been the place where I'd hidden myself away, playing my secret games among the packing cases and lines of drying washing and occasional scuttling mice. I had read Grandpa's books down there, savouring them and the damp smell of washing and the beating rain. And when Mum had died I had gone down there again, to shed my secret tears beneath the empty lines. I hadn't been down since. I shouldn't have gone down there now.

I put my cocoa on the sill and looked out at eye-level upon the lawn. The room was dark. I liked it like that. I found my favourite armchair, Grandpa's one with the broken arm, and settled in it and ate my biscuit and sipped the cocoa.

I couldn't help but think of Mum, who some people might have thought was dull like me, but I knew had been the best mum in the world. She'd had pure sunshine in her eyes and her soft brown hair, and she was always smiling, always full of fun.

I remembered the Christmas game she used to make us play – even Dad, who was too old, too busy, and too stuffy to have time for fun. A riddle it had been, with family jokes in it that changed from year to year, and a prize at the end for the first of us to work it out. Dad would cry, 'Oh, Jane, not *another* of your awful games . . .!' But he always joined in with Grandpa and me, and sometimes even won.

I would catch Mum's eye, and I knew she'd let him win. We understood each other, Mum and I.

We were different to Dad, and like each other – in all sorts of ways.

It was she who introduced me to the Guildhall garden, where we picked crocuses in spring. She who showed me where the swans nested by Tyger Pool. I remember us watching them on the pool, and the dragonflies skimming its surface, and her saying, 'It hasn't changed since I was a little girl. This is a grand town.'

Oh, I hoped that where she'd gone was grand too. It surely had to be, for someone as good as Mum. Down the side of the chair, I felt the photograph, which I'd buried there because I couldn't bear it by my bed any more. Even in the dark, I could see her in the frame, smiling up at me. I didn't need the light to know that I was hand in hand with her, five years old, dressed up for our first separation – school.

I thrust the photograph back down the chair and stumbled from the utility, back upstairs leaving the rest of the cocoa, and my memories, behind. I climbed into bed, pulling the covers over me and wondering why I had gone down there.

When I awoke again, Christmas had well-and-truly dawned, with sleet falling from a grubby and dispirited sky onto a ground where the frost had disappeared, as if by magic, as if it had never been.

There wasn't much for the angels to sing hosannahs about this year. Just Miss Vine's stooping figure on the pavement, half-hidden beneath her umbrella as she answered Emmanuel's ringing communion call. Just me dropping Father Christmas's joyless presents on the floor.

Later in the morning Miss Vine called, bearing a card and a pot of hyacinths. She wore a yellow dress, with a wonky hem. I remember staring at her pudding-basin hair, and her hands which were lined from gardening.

'Stay and have a sherry,' Dad said awkwardly. Down Planetree Avenue, Miss Vine was like God and the Queen rolled into one – a remote, mysterious creature as far as most people were concerned, whom everybody tiptoed around with immense respect, although looking at the shabby state of her, nobody knew why.

'You must let me know,' she told Dad after the funeral, 'if there's anything that I can do.'

Dad had thanked her stiffly, but he'd made it so plain that he was managing, that apart from once taking Grandpa in for a cup of tea, and sending him home with a fruit cake, she left us alone. Until today.

Now she said that she really wouldn't stay, and before Dad could protest, out of politeness, the doorbell rang again, and it was the Cutlers.

I had been dreading their visit for weeks. Usually they took a Christmas break somewhere nice and warm, but this year, as Maple Cutler had complained in school, they were sacrificing themselves because of Dad and me. Sacrificing themselves! It was plain from the minute they came in, driving Miss Vine away, that they had forced themselves on us out of curiosity. They wanted to see if we were coping.

Dad ushered them into our front room, which looked as crisp and orderly as a freshly decorated cake before the first cut spoils everything. Mrs Cutler's dark eyes pored over it. You could see her disappointment.

'What will you drink?' Dad said, in his cheery Father Christmas voice. I almost expected him to say, 'Ho, ho, ho!'

'I'll have a sherry. Bob drinks whisky,' Mrs Cutler said.

'But anything will do,' Mr Cutler added nervously.

Dad handed out the drinks. Mrs Cutler said how nice it was not to be responsible for the turkey, she hated cooking Christmas lunch. Maple, next to Grandpa on the settee, crossed her fish-net legs which were destined for the pages of some glossy magazine, once it had 'found' her. She yawned, bored. But she wasn't bored for long!

'Cheers!' Grandpa said, tipping his drink down his best fancy waistcoat, and in a sideways spasm over Maple's stockinged legs.

She sprang to her feet. I laughed. I couldn't help myself, even when Dad glared at me. 'He ought to be in a home!' she cried, no doubt repeating what her parents said. Mrs Cutler dabbed at her with a handkerchief, but Maple pushed her away. She rushed off to the bathroom.

'You should have someone in the house to help you with him,' Mrs Cutler said, as if Grandpa wasn't there, and couldn't hear her. 'He's becoming a liability. You can't carry on like this on your own, Georgie dear.'

Dad – whom not even Mum would have called 'Georgie dear' – extracted Grandpa's waistcoat from him, and went to rinse it at the kitchen sink.

'We're managing just fine,' he said. His face was white. I hoped he wouldn't lose his temper. He didn't often – but when he did everybody knew about it!

Maybe Mr Cutler thought so too. Without looking at his wife, he said, 'I warned you, dear. The old boy's all he's got of *her* now – apart from Rosemary, of course. You've got to be careful what you say.'

'Someone's got to point these things out,' Mrs Cutler said, as if she was a woman with a mission.

Mr Cutler downed his drink and helped himself to another one. Dad called us through for lunch. The colour had returned to his cheeks but, hardly surprisingly, the meal wasn't a success. Mrs Cutler scarcely stopping talking, and Maple scowled and so did I. Mr Cutler emptied glass after glass of wine, and the dining room seemed empty – despite the table being full on each side – and our voices sounded hollow and unreal.

I thought that if Mrs Cutler said, once more, that lunch was every bit as nice as it would have been if they'd gone away, I'd strangle her. I thought that if Mr Cutler laughed that silly laugh of his again, I'd strangle him.

'Oh, Bob, not the government on Christmas Day,' his wife interrupted him on the only occasion when he seemed to have something to say.

After lunch, Dad washed up and cleaned out the sink and draining-board until they shone.

18

Though it was Christmas Day he couldn't let his standards go – or let anybody help! He liked the house to be clean as a new pin, and he liked to get on with it alone. Mum would have extracted him from the kitchen, made him sit down and put up his feet, but she wasn't here, was she?

'It's time for the Queen's speech,' Mrs Cutler trilled.

Dad brought in a pot of tea. I excused myself. Grandpa had gone up to his room. I thought I'd join him. I'd had enough of what the Cutlers no doubt thought was neighbourliness!

'Perhaps Maple would like to come with you,' Dad said. He seemed to think she was my friend. I don't know why. I pulled a face at her, which Mrs Cutler saw, and left her to the Queen's speech and her mother's conversation.

It was a relief to get away. Grandpa lay asleep upon his bed. I squeezed round it and opened the window, desperate for fresh air. All down the row everything was quiet as though the whole network of roads was listening to the Queen's speech. They'd probably all talked about the government through lunch, I thought, and would settle down when the speech was done, to sleep in front of the film matinée.

My eyes came to rest on the Guildhall garden. A silver balloon was caught in a tree, and a bicycle leaned against the end wall. It wasn't one of the old frames that people threw over there, when they used the Guildhall garden as a rubbish dump, but a shining bike with a bright blue saddle. Next to it stood a tree in a pot, and a netball post.

19

The balloon dislodged itself. It bounced across the garden, and I saw other things that hadn't been there before – a lawnmower, a trailer full of coal, the back end of a van emerging from what once had been a garage.

I would have laughed out loud, if Grandpa hadn't been asleep. As it was, I left him to it and hurried downstairs. I'd got it wrong, hadn't I, about the ghost. The Cutlers mightn't know it yet, but they had neighbours at long last. Neighbours! I was overwhelmed with curiosity. Who, I asked myself, would move into a run-down place like the Old Guildhall, after dark on Christmas Eve?

Filled with the urge to find out, I crept past the front room. I could hear the television, and Mrs Cutler talking over it. She was saying, 'Your Rosemary's lacking a woman about the house, already. You can just tell.' I didn't know how she dared.

Relieved to get away from her, I crept out of the back door, and down our garden. I squeezed through the Guildhall's fence, certain that nobody would see me. It was getting dark, and I knew all the hiding places anyway.

Carefully, I picked my path. Lights were on in the big hall, but laughter came from the end of the building. I followed it. Round a corner, next to the side door, I came across a window which I hadn't noticed before. Maybe it had been boarded up.

The laughter was coming through the window. Astonished at my boldness, I dropped onto my hands and knees. I shuffled under the stone sill, and raised my head slowly. I found myself staring at a dresser stacked with half-unpacked crockery, a black stove with saucepans on it, a candlelit table covered with plates and food, and a family.

They sat around the table. The dad was doling out the Christmas pudding. He was a huge man, with thick hair and a bushy beard. His hands hacked away with the knife, like an inept Viking warrior.

Next to him, the mum dolloped out thick custard. She wore white dungarees out of which her stomach ballooned as if she were an incarnation of the Virgin Mary. I looked at her silvery, sticking-up hair. Of course – she had been the ghost of Christmas! What a fool I was! She paused to stroke her stomach. The boy at the end of the table made her laugh.

He was swinging back on his chair, an older boy than me, with long fair hair – thick like his dad's – and a yellow jumper with holes in it, and the most amazing smile that I had ever seen.

Next to him, sat a girl who was as dark as he was fair. Her mountain of hair fell over her face. She was eating quietly, head down.

I stared at them as though they were actors, spotlit by their candle on the Guildhall's stage. Who were they? Where had they come from? I watched them eating. I watched them laugh. When they'd finished, they took up the candle, and left the room. The girl switched off the light. All the way through the meal, she was the one who had remained quiet.

I wanted to know why. I wanted to know everything. Sleet was falling, but I didn't care. I ran

21

round the building after them, and there they were again. I peered through one of the windows of the big hall. They were settling themselves around a log fire, amid rolls of carpet, settees, tables, mattresses, pictures in frames. . . .

'It's time to do the tree,' the dad said, producing a box of matches and shaking it.

They had placed a tree in an ornamental tub – not a Christmas tree, but an ordinary one, which they had cut down. On its bare branches they'd hung silver balls and coloured lights and candles.

'It won't be the same,' the girl said wistfully.

'Come on, Viola,' the dad said. 'We can't go back. We've got to look ahead.'

Reluctantly, she took the matches. He turned off the main light and, in the small remaining glow, I saw him squeeze her arm. Silently, she began lighting the candles. Each one changed the tree, adding to its shadow on the wall. Finally, the whole thing was aflame.

The family clapped, but it seemed to me that the girl had made them sad, too. She dropped to her knees underneath the tree, and wound a handle in the side of the tub. It began rotating slowly. I could hear the tinkling of a Christmas tune. The tree revolved, the tune played, the candles winked.

'And now for our game,' the mother said.

There were groans and catcalls. 'We can't go through a single Christmas without one of your wretched games,' the dad said.

It went straight through me. One too many echoes from my own home – a whisper from an age that couldn't be brought back again. My own dad, who used to say it just like that, my own mum who'd gone. . . .

Suddenly, as much as I'd wanted to be near them, I wanted to get away. Down the garden I stumbled, through the awful sleet, through the broken fence, into the stream bed. I didn't want their laughter, and their secret sadness, and their awful games which made me fear them more than angels and ghosts.

I closed my eyes to shut them out. But round and round, inside my head, went their wretched Christmas tree. And, full of promises, its candles winked at me.

3

I longed to get back to school, which was unusual
for me, but it wasn't only Christmas which had got
me down. Something was happening to Grandpa.
He slept half the day as if it were night and woke
us nightly, crashing about the house trying to find
the bathroom, which he said had moved. One
time, I went into his room and he was weeping. I
asked him why, but he wouldn't say. He called me
Jane. I told him I was Rosemary. He stared at me, as
if we'd never met before.

Gloom gripped the whole house. There was no
escape from it. Even Dad's brisk company didn't
help. Every morning he devised a fresh plan of
chores to be done, and he'd pull apart the house
and wouldn't let me help him put it back again,
saying I wouldn't do it properly.

So, when the new term began, I was up early for
it, into my grey uniform without a word of com-
plaint and downstairs for breakfast with my hair
brushed and shoes shining and bag packed. Afterwards, I was down those front steps without looking
back.

'Goodbye,' called Dad, washing up the breakfast

things with an apron tied over his office suit, for he was back to work too.

I ran off, trying not to worry about whether Grandpa would be all right alone. It was pouring with rain. Up Planetree Avenue I hurried, to the main road. When I reached the corner, the bus was about to pull away from outside the Old Guildhall. The driver saw me, and waited. I squeezed in. My wet umbrella dripped on my feet and on the feet of the two people next to me. I was wedged in so tight that I couldn't help it.

When we pulled away, I realized that they were the boy and girl from the Old Guildhall. They were waving to their mum, who stood at the gate, watching them go. The girl's face was white, and she clutched her school bag tightly. Her dark hair was tied into a plait, but already bits of it were working loose around her face. The velvet pinafore frock she wore beneath her coat, with its embroidered yoke and bits of ribbon, was nothing like our uniform.

Her brother tried to reassure her with his bright smile.

'He'll get on all right,' I thought, despite his unkempt hair and equally non-regulation clothes.

After registration, the girl was brought into our room, and introduced as Viola Rocket. The whole class tittered. What a name! She was given to Maple to take care of – I can't imagine why, apart from Miss Parker being too stupid to know better. Maple laughed at her behind her back all day, and Viola said nothing, just sat in silence, except when Miss Parker made her stand up.

'Tell us all about yourself,' she said, trying to sound welcoming.

Viola glared at her. 'We used to live on a farm, but we had to give it up,' she said. 'Now my dad does whatever jobs come along, and we rent the Old Guildhall on Whiteley Hill. Is that the sort of thing you want to know?'

There was an electric silence. Miss Parker actually blushed. 'Really, Viola,' she said. 'I'm sure I didn't mean. . . .'

Viola stuck out her chin, but tears glittered in the corner of her eyes. Sniggers ran round the classroom.

'Sit down,' Miss Parker said, trying to regain her composure.

We came out together at the end of the day. Viola's brother was waiting for her. The bus came along, and we piled on. They sat a couple of seats in front of me. To my surprise, Maple Cutler came and joined me. It wasn't me, though, that she was interested in. 'He's *never* her boyfriend?' she said, none-too-quietly.

'He's her *brother*,' I said, feeling superior for once. 'Didn't you know?'

She didn't answer me. Her eyes narrowed. You could see that she was planning. When we got off the bus, she flashed Viola her front-page smile – which was a change from what she'd given her all day! 'See you tomorrow,' she said silkily.

Viola turned in her gate as if she hadn't heard.

But the boy heard, and smiled back. Which, of course, was what Maple wanted.

'Ridley? Viola? How did it go?' I heard their mum calling through the open kitchen door.

'Oh, Mum, I hate it here,' Viola replied. 'I hate the whole town.'

The door closed behind them. We were left alone. 'Well!' said Maple. 'Who does she think she is?'

'It must be difficult when you're new,' I said, sticking up for Viola Rocket, although I didn't know why.

Maple wasn't interested. She hurried up her path without another word, sending the 'B & B & Evening Meal' sign spinning in her eagerness to get indoors, no doubt to perfect the plan which would capture Ridley Rocket. Ridley Rocket! With a name like that, and Maple in pursuit, I started feeling sorry for him.

When I got home, Grandpa's door was shut, as if he were asleep. I retired to my bedroom to do my homework. Before I'd got very far, however, he appeared in the doorway, wearing two pairs of trousers and clutching a dusty copy of the *Encyclopaedia Britannica* to his chest.

'Is that for me?' I said. Grandpa was always trying to help me with my homework.

'I can't open it,' he said, poking the book as though it were a cornflake box. 'I can't find the milk. I can't find where your mother keeps the apricots.'

'It's teatime, Grandpa,' I said, gently taking the book from him before he broke its spine, 'not breakfast time. You've been asleep all day.'

Grandpa's brightness faded clean away, and the look on his face went through me. It was as if the old Grandpa was in there somewhere, the sharp Grandpa with the black eyes who knew what books were for all right, and he was looking out at the befuddled Grandpa with too many trousers on, understanding what was going on but unable to stop it.

'Let's go down and watch the telly, Grandpa,' I said helplessly. 'Dad'll be in soon to do the tea, but I could make some toast if you wanted me to.'

He didn't want me to. I made him comfortable on the settee, and he held my hand so tightly that I had to stay, perched on the arm until Dad came home, with a briefcase full of work to do later.

In the night, Grandpa woke us again, with another expedition through the house. There was something about the attic room, up on the lonely top floor, with its spiky shadows. You could imagine anything up there. Curled up tight in my bed with my head buried, I imagined that my beloved, crashing, grumbling Grandpa downstairs had turned into a monster. Which in a way, I suppose, he had.

Dad directed Grandpa back to bed, but I couldn't sleep. I got up, and sat on the windowsill. The lights were out in the Old Guildhall. I thought about Viola, and wondered if she was sleeping. I could understand her hating school, but why had she got it in for the whole town? I thought of Tyger

Pool with its swans and lilies and dragonflies, and Whiteley Wood with its ancient trees. Maybe it was something to do with Grandpa, but anger rose in me. I couldn't be cross with him, I loved him too much. But I could be cross with her. Who did she think she was, despising our town?

'Give her a chance,' a voice inside me said. 'You don't know what her reasons are.'

But anger doesn't accept reasons, however good they are.

One way or another, there was no getting away from Viola Rocket for weeks. She and her brother were the star-turns in school, what with their unusual adaptations of our uniform, and her aloof ways, and his easy, contrasting smile, which made everyone want to be friends with him.

Mrs Rocket was a star-turn too. She took to waiting for them after school, looking like some sort of refugee in a coat of rainbow colours and a scarf twisted around her sticking-up hair, knotted at the top, and hanging over her eye. Her pregnant bulge stuck out so far that it defied the laws of gravity.

Mr Rocket came for them sometimes too, in his beaten-up old van which looked as if it had done a tour of all the tips in town, its roofrack laden with acquisitions of every shape and size. He had this way of smiling, just like Ridley. You'd never have known that they were newcomers. They seemed to have made friends all over town. I didn't know how they had managed it.

Winter was beginning to melt away. There were

snowdrops in the garden and buds on the plane tree outside our house. I remember looking at those buds which I'd thought I'd never see again. I'd felt as though the winter into which we'd been plunged when Mum had died, was going to last for the rest of my life. . . .

One Saturday, to escape Dad's spring-cleaning, I struggled down the windswept road to Whiteley Wood to feed my friends, the swans. I hadn't been down there for weeks. I passed the War Memorial and slid between the trees. It was good to be back. Abandoning the made-up path, I pushed down through the budding undergrowth, crunching over the woodland floor. I was so happy. I didn't notice anything at first. I loved this ancient wood, every bit of it.

Only when I reached Tyger Pool did I see the new fence, and the sign on it:

PRIVATE LAND
THIS SITE HAS BEEN DESIGNATED FOR
REDEVELOPMENT
KEEP OUT

The fence went right the way round the pool, enclosing the trees at the end of it and a whole slice of wood up towards the new dual carriageway on the other side. I stared at it in astonishment. Private land? Redevelopment? A shiver, as if of electricity, ran through me.

'Are you all right?'

Viola Rocket was standing in front of me, collar turned up against the wind, holding bread for the swans too. 'Do you want to sit down?' she said anxiously. I must have looked a real sight.

'What are they doing to the pool?' I said. I couldn't believe my eyes.

'They're draining it,' she said. 'Didn't you know?'

I hadn't known, but now I did. In a rush, Mum's words came back to me: 'This is a grand town.' What would the swans and dragonflies and lilies do now? What would I do?

'They can't drain it!' I said. 'Look at it. It's bottomless!'

'They're going to build houses,' Viola said implacably.

I stared at the dark pool, hating her, hating everything, most of all hating change.

'It's not my fault,' she said. 'I like it down here, too. It's the only thing I do like in this horrid town.'

I turned. She looked so sad that I could tell she meant it. Suddenly I found myself telling her about the forges that had been built all the way down this valley, right from the moors to the centre of town. I told her about the mills that had long-since gone, though their pools remained. We looked together into the dark water. Grandpa said that Tyger Pool was as ancient as the lake into which Excalibur returned. 'It's been here for centuries,' I said. I wasn't angry with Viola any more.

She listened to me, hair blowing in the wind, face solemn, head nodding. When I left the pool, she followed me. We climbed up towards the War Memorial. Ahead of us, a couple of boys on bikes raced by, laughing as if it didn't matter that everything was going to change.

I imagined the wood full of ghosts – the angry ghosts of all the people who'd enjoyed walking in it, and the indignant ghosts of those to whom it had belonged, long years before our town. The cold wind blew. Out of the corner of my eye, I could see the pool scuffing up. It looked angry and grey, and the shaking trees looked angry too. I imagined the water saying, 'There are some things better left untouched!' and the trees complaining, 'After all we've done for you. . . .'

Viola must have felt it too. Suddenly, she began to run, and without a word I did too – past the War Memorial, up our road, not stopping until we reached my gate against which we leaned, panting and companionable, bound by something we couldn't quite explain.

When she regained her breath, Viola said, 'You can come round to my house, if you like,' diffidently, as if it didn't matter either way.

But she wouldn't offer again, and I knew it. We'd been thrown together suddenly, but she'd change back to her old self on Monday when she climbed into that pinafore dress of hers. And I'd change too.

'Do you really mean it?' I said, as if I couldn't believe that anyone wanted to be friends with me.

She grinned wickedly. I'd never seen her smile before. It completely transformed her face. 'You'll make a change from Maple Cutler chasing after Ridley!' she said. 'Come on. Of course I do.'

4

We ducked under a washing-line, upon which hung tiny socks and vests, embroidered night-dresses and little blankets.

'Mum's getting ready for the new baby,' Viola explained. She opened the side door. 'Come in.'

I entered the untidiest kitchen I had ever seen. Dusty cups and saucers were piled up on the dresser, along with unopened letters in brown envelopes, jam pots and odd gloves. Dirty dishes filled the sink. Black bin bags lined the floor, waiting to be put out. I listened. The house was silent.

'They must have gone out,' Viola said, watching my eyes flitting about. 'I'll make some coffee, then I'll show you around. It's a funny old place – but you can see that for yourself. Dad says it's got potential but the rest of us aren't so sure!'

She put the kettle on the stove and washed a few dishes while she waited for it to boil. I savoured the smells of the house – coal dust, garlic, coffee, herbs. Despite its untidiness, it felt cosy and welcoming.

The kettle boiled, and she made our coffees.

'Come on,' she said, leading me down three

stone steps at the far end of the room. 'Careful – mind the last one. It's broken.'

We passed through a dark doorway into a windowless room, full of dank smells. She switched on a light and I saw that we were sandwiched in tight between a low, rough-wood ceiling, held up by huge iron beams, and a damp stone floor. The room was full of bags of cement and bits of timber and tools.

'One of Dad's projects,' Viola said airily. 'He's going to turn it into a living-room. We're under the old stage. It's a bit hard to imagine but come into the hall and then you'll see.'

She led me up more steps at the end of the room and through a door in what turned out to be the front of the stage. We found ourselves in the big hall. In contrast with the room we'd left it was very bright, with light streaming through the windows and walls that rose, uninterrupted, right up to the high roof. It was just as full of tables, chairs, mattresses, rolls of carpet and pictures in frames as I remembered it from Christmas Day .

'You've still got your tree—' I began to say, but an urgent voice interrupted me.

'Viola? Is that you?!' it called.

I couldn't figure out where it came from. Somewhere above my head.

'Mum?' Viola said. 'I thought you had gone out. Are you all right?'

'Viola, oh VIOLA!' the voice cried with relief.

Viola dropped her coffee cup. It smashed on the floor. 'I'm coming, Mum. I'm coming,' she cried. 'It's all right, Mum! I'm here.'

She climbed onto the stage and plunged between its velvet curtains. I followed her, caught up in it all. In the dark, behind the curtains, I stumbled into some sort of metal frame, which rose up from the stage like scaffolding.

I let out a yelp of pain. Viola switched on a light. I saw beds, screens, wardrobes, chests of drawers and, in the midst of them, Mrs Rocket lying on her back, clutching a screwed-up eiderdown as if it were a teddy bear, against her chest.

What was wrong with her? At first I thought her hands were speckled with blood, but then I noticed the pots and brushes on the floor and the daubs of purple paint on the wall behind the beds.

'You know how slow Dad is at getting things done . . .' she joked. Her eyes were bulging. 'I was just trying to hurry things along. Oh God, *hurry things along* – Viola, come and hold my *hand*! *Why . . . do these things . . . always happen . . . to me..!?*'

She buried her chin in the eiderdown and her face went as purple as the paint on the wall. Viola grabbed her hand, as she was bidden. I would have run, but I was stuck. I couldn't move. I felt like an intruder, a Peeping-Tom, ashamed of myself – but all I could do was stare.

For, right in front of me, to my amazement, Viola's baby sister, Eloise Rocket, was being born.

I didn't know that birth could be like that. I'd somehow got the idea that it required machinery to bring a child into the world, operated by starched nurses in sterile masks and caps.

But here was Viola's mother, screaming and pushing and laughing – laughing! I swear she was! – all on her own, and when the baby came out and began to cry, we could see that she was happy.

Happy! How could she be happy after something like that? How could she lie back stroking her sticky child as if everything was all right?

'Go to the kitchen and phone the doctor, Viola,' she said, wiping her tears away. 'The number's on the pad.'

Viola couldn't move. She was stuck even faster than I had been. 'I'll go,' I volunteered.

By the time I got to the phone, I was shaking all over. I held onto the receiver as tightly as I could.

'I'm on my way!' the doctor said.

When I returned, the three of them were wrapped up in the eiderdown, on Mrs Rocket's bed.

'Doctor's coming,' I said.

Mrs Rocket smiled gratefully. She lifted back the eiderdown for me to see. 'This is Ellie Rocket,' she said, as though I were an old friend and not a stranger.

I looked at Ellie Rocket lying there, so tiny, so waxy and sweet.

'Have you ever seen anything so wonderful?' Mrs Rocket said.

A new-born baby, minutes old, black-eyed, black-haired, full of strange, new life. '*Never,*' I said.

Swinging on the gate, however, waiting for the doctor, my excitement began to be replaced by anxiety. Maybe it was the cold wind that was getting to me. But what if something went wrong? What if Ellie Rocket died?

The doctor's car pulled up. She came running from it, with the midwife right behind her.

'Where is she?' they cried.

'Follow me,' I said, jumping off the gate.

The next half-hour was spent running up and down with hot water, baby clothes, the midwife's bags of equipment, and the 'nice cup of tea' they seemed to think Mrs Rocket needed. Baby Eloise was washed, the cord was cut which joined her to her mother, and she was dressed in clothes which made her look like an ordinary baby. I began to stop worrying that she would die.

An electric fire was switched on and Mrs Rocket was washed as if she were a baby too. The doctor scolded her for not making it to the hospital in time. She said she'd come back tonight, to make sure everything was all right. She climbed off the stage, helped down by me, and stood brushing the dust from her suit, looking as if she'd never seen such a pickle in her life before. But the midwife went on, serenely washing Viola's mother, as if she attended to women in these circumstances every day.

'And where's the father?' the doctor said, looking up and down the big hall, as if she expected him to appear like a rabbit from a conjurer's hat.

'Here I am,' said Mr Rocket – and she nearly died of shock. He came bursting through the doors in the front of the stage. 'Who are you?' he said. 'And why do you want to know?'

The doctor bridled. You could tell she wasn't impressed. 'While you were out,' she said, pronouncing the word 'out' as if it were a crime, 'your wife has delivered. You have a child.'

'I have a WHAT?' Mr Rocket said.

'A daughter,' the doctor said.

He took us all in – the doctor, me, the midwife washing Mrs Rocket, Viola nursing something on her lap. He took in the empty cot before the electric fire. Then, instead of what we all expected, WHAT HAVE YOU DONE?' he bawled at Mrs Rocket. 'YOU'VE RUINED THE WHOLE STAGE! WHO WANTS *PURPLE* WALLS!?'

To my surprise, Viola's mother laughed. 'Oh, Jim!' she cried, as if she understood something about him which was lost on the rest of us. The baby began to whimper. She reached for her and held her. 'Here she is!' she called.

It was an awesome sight, watching Mr Rocket bounding onto the stage and falling upon his new child like a hungry beast. In a couple of strides he was right across it and his great arms took first the baby into them, and then his wife.

'Trust you to go and do it like this!' he said, holding her tight.

'I'm sorry about the purple walls,' she said, and they both burst out laughing.

When the midwife and doctor had departed, we left Mrs Rocket and Ellie to sleep, and went down to the kitchen to make what Mr Rocket called 'our celebratory feast' out of slabs of bread, and jam and honey, and a hunk of cheese.

Ridley came bursting in, halfway through. His face was a picture when Viola told him what he'd missed. 'Is Mum all right?' he said. He looked horrified. You'd have thought that something terrible had happened.

'They're both asleep,' his father said. 'They're fine. You can see them later. Sit down and eat.'

We all ate. Mr Rocket whipped up milky coffees on the stove. Viola told Ridley what had happened in graphic detail. He pleaded with her to stop. 'You're a wimp!' she crowed.

He protested, and we all laughed. I never once thought about going home. I had forgotten it, forgotten everything outside these four walls. Ellie's birth had turned me upside down. I had even forgotten what was happening down in Whiteley Wood.

We finished eating and set upon the kitchen. I washed the dirty dishes in the sink and put out the bin bags and cut up the vegetables for a stew. Ridley wrote a note for the milkman. It said:

> HIP! HIP! HOORAY!
> WE'RE GOING TO NEED MORE MILK
> AFTER TODAY!
> 6 PINTS PLEASE!!

I laughed at him and he laughed back at me. Could this be me? I asked myself.

Mr Rocket came into the kitchen. 'They're not warm enough up there,' he said. 'There's a howling draught coming from the big hall, even when the curtains are drawn. Tell you what we'll do—' he pushed the table close to the sink, to make a gap beside the stove '—We'll put a bed here. What do you think?'

It sounded like a good idea – until we tried to move the bed. It might have been cast iron, it weighed so much. We hauled it up from the big hall, piece by piece. Mr Rocket erected it. Ridley and I pulled a mountainous feather mattress over the springs.

Viola found some clean laundry and made it up, throwing over the top of it a cotton counterpane with long tassles. It looked ridiculous, that huge bed right in the middle of the floor. But the stove was crackling with fire and the room was lovely and warm.

'I'll go and fetch them,' Mr Rocket said.

I would have liked to be enthroned as though I were a queen in that bed in the very centre of the kitchen. Mrs Rocket collapsed into it, wearing a fresh nightdress, cream-coloured like the counterpane, with her silvery hair brushed so that it lay flat against her head. The whole bed creaked, but Baby Ellie didn't wake as Mr Rocket laid her by her mother's side.

'Thank you,' Mrs Rocket said. She smiled at us all and closed her eyes.

'I ought to go home,' I said, suddenly remembering Dad. He would be worrying himself silly about where I'd been.

'Have you got to?' Viola said. It felt as though the party was over. We stared at each other awkwardly. I was one of them for now – but it would never be the same again. 'Ask her dad to let her stay,' she pleaded. 'Ask if she can sleep the night.'

'We could try,' Mr Rocket said, with an easy shrug. 'That is, if Rosemary would like to. . . .'

Like to? Of course I would! I'd never been invited to sleep at a friend's house before. 'But I'll be in the way,' I said, astonished at this family, so different to mine, with no apparent sense of privacy.

'Be in the way?' Mr Rocket said. 'Of course you won't!'

He beamed at me and I felt warm and welcome. I never wanted to go home. Unfortunately, however, Dad would never let me stay.

I didn't know Mr Rocket, though!

'Your daughter's been a *marvel*,' he enthused when he, Viola and I stood before Dad, explaining where I had been, and what had happened, and why it was so vital that I should stay. 'She absolutely saved the day. She's so sensible. So mature. You must be proud of her. We wondered, could she stay? Just overnight. We'll send her back first thing in the morning. If Viola has a friend it'll keep her out of our way. You know what girls are like when they get together. . . .'

I'm sure Dad didn't but, 'Well, perhaps . . .' he said, unable to resist Mr Rocket's devastating smile, and Viola's, '*Please, oh please*. . . .'

That evening, Viola showed me Brick Barns for

42

the first time. We were lying on our beds, ready for the night, whispering. There was a storm building up outside, but inside everything seemed grave and still.

I looked at the stone house in Viola's photograph, and the barns behind it, and the pines and the rolling hills. They were so beautiful. Now I understood why she stared out of the classroom window, as if none of us were there. Now I knew why she hated our town!

'I'm so sorry,' I said.

'This isn't our home,' she whispered, bitterly.

Astonished at myself, I began to tell her about Mum. I couldn't look her in the eye but I told her it all, right down to what Grandpa used to be like in the old days, before she had gone.

'I never want to get old and die,' I said.

'Neither do I,' she said, turning out the light.

I lay in the dark, worn out by the day. The wind beat in waves against the Guildhall's walls. I looked at the velvet curtains swaying in the draught, and snuggled down the bed to keep warm. Between the curtains, I could just make out the outline of the metal frame on which I'd scraped my knee. It stretched across the stage from side to side, and arched above our heads.

'What *is* that thing?' I said, yawning.

'Dad's going to repair it,' Viola replied. 'One of his projects . . . window-frame . . . find new glass . . . cut out all the draughts. . . .' And she was asleep, just like that.

I, too, drifted to sleep. But in the blackness of it, the broken frame remained. There was something beyond it where the hall should have been, and I couldn't see what, but I was frightened. It was as though there were eyes on me. And that wasn't all. A smell rose to greet me. It was like meat burning at the bottom of an angry, bubbling stew. It was *horrible*.

I woke up with a start. I was on the floor with all the bedcovers on top of me. Hard rain drummed on the earth outside. I climbed back into bed, trying to laugh at myself. What a thing to dream, on this stage where I had witnessed new life! I closed my eyes, tight. Sleep snuffed me out like a candle. I remembered no more.

5

The storm was still blowing in the morning. Not that the Rockets were bothered by it, shut away behind the Guildhall's impregnable walls. Mrs Rocket lay serenely upon her bed, directing breakfast. Baby Ellie fed from her breast as if there were no tomorrow, all that mattered was *now*.

I would have stayed with them for ever, if I could. But I had promised Dad to go home first thing. And in any case, something from my dream was lingering. I wouldn't have admitted it but I wanted to make sure that everything was all right.

And it *was* all right – or so I first thought. The house was cold and empty but there was nothing special about that. We ate breakfast in silence, but then we always did when Grandpa slept late.

It was only slowly that I sensed something unusual in the air. There was an *atmosphere*, which I had never felt before. Dad was as bleak as I'd seen him since Mum had gone. He was taut enough to snap. All day long he rushed about the house, apparently busy but seeming to get nowhere. When he came into my room that night, I shut my eyes and pretended to sleep. I couldn't stand any more of him.

But even when he had gone, the tension remained. I lay listening to the storm, which was as wild as the night before, imagining that I could hear a frantic message in the rhythm of the beating wind and rain.

When I awoke next day, the sky was bright blue. The air was absolutely still. There were broken branches all over our garden, and the lawn was waterlogged. I didn't know why the passing of a storm should make such a difference, but the tension had gone.

Viola and I rode to school in the back of Mr Rocket's van, which smelt of wood chippings, and leaking petrol, and soap. The baby was wonderful, Mrs Rocket was fine. We saw Ridley pushing his bicycle, with Maple by his side. We both laughed.

All day, I had the strangest sense of calm. Looking back, it was like a lull before the real storm. At the end of it, I came home alone. Instead of taking the bus with Viola, I walked through Whiteley Wood.

The trees were motionless, as if worn out with all that shaking. Tyger Pool was silvery and still. It might have been a painted scene, so ornamental were the swans as they glided on its surface, which was just like mirror-glass.

I didn't know why I'd come this way. The wood seemed secretive and remote from me now. I didn't want to see the fence, or its awful sign, whose message seemed to come after me from tree to tree – seemed to follow me.

'It isn't *my* fault they're building here,' I said, as if – with no one else to pin it on – the wood was accusing me. 'It's nothing to do with me.'

When I got indoors, to my surprise, I smelt the beginnings of tea.

'Is that you, Dad?' I called curiously – for wasn't he meant to be working?

Before anyone could answer, the door bell rang. I span around, surprised. I hadn't seen a single soul on the pavement. Who could it be? I looked at the outline of a figure, through the glass. It was me who did it. Me who opened the door. . . .

If the coming of the Rockets to the Old Guildhall changed my life for ever, then this did too. I forgot Whiteley Wood and Tyger Pool. I forgot my new friends, the Rockets, even Baby Ellie whom I'd watched being born. I forgot my ups, my downs, my likes, my dislikes, Grandpa, awful Maple Cutler, *everything*.

'You've been expecting me.'

A woman stood on the doorstep. She had pale eyes, wore a see-through plastic mac, and carried a suitcase.

I stared at her in surprise. 'I don't think so,' I said. 'You must have the wrong address.'

'I don't think I have,' she said, and before I knew what was happening, Dad came rushing along the hall, smoothing down his jacket and straightening his tie, passing me by as if I wasn't even there.

'*Welcome*,' he said. He stood there looking at her. His face was white. It was a funny moment.

'Can you help me with my things?' the woman said. There was a musical lilt to her voice but I couldn't place the accent which was soft and low.

Dad shook himself. 'Yes, of course,' he said. He took her suitcase, and a carrier bag containing a plant, and a birdcage which was so heavy that he had to put it down again, just inside the door. 'Is that everything?'

'It is, for now,' the woman said. She removed the cover from the cage to reveal a bird of some sort: a bedraggled, ugly little thing, with scrawny feathers. I didn't know what it was. Some sort of foreign bird, maybe?

'Would you like to see the room?' Dad said. 'It's this way.'

She nodded and her hair bobbed. It was pale, like her eyes, and sandy coloured like the few freckles on her skin. 'Anything you say,' she said, smiling to reveal the whitest teeth I had ever seen.

I followed them down to the utility. *My* utility where the fruits of Dad's hard work were plain to see. The clutter had been cleared away, and the floor had been carpeted with a rug I'd never seen, and Grandpa's old furniture had been polished for the first time in years, and rearranged. All that remained of the way things used to be, was the chair below the window – the chair with the broken arm, down which Mum's photograph was stuffed.

An electric fire had been brought down and switched on to warm the room, and the window which looked at eye-level onto the lawn, had been covered with net curtains and a plastic Venetian blind. You couldn't see out of it any more.

Dad showed the woman how the blind went up and down, and where the light switch was. When he switched it on, what for years had been a bare bulb was swathed in a fringed shade.

The woman smiled again. 'It's perrfect,' she said. She had this way of rolling her 'r's', which made her sound like a purring kitten. She brought out a wallet and unfolded money from it which she offered to Dad. He took the notes, and if I hadn't understood before, I did now. We had taken in what Mrs Cutler would have called a 'paying guest'.

A paying guest.

I never would have thought it possible. What had come over Dad – Dad, who was obsessional about his privacy! And why hadn't he consulted me? I clenched my teeth, grinding them so hard that he couldn't help but notice me.

'Ah, Rosemary,' he said, smiling treacherously. 'We have a guest. She'll be here every afternoon when you get home from school. She'll share our kitchen, so you'll have to make room for her, and be a good girl, and help her to find her way around. This is Rosemary, Miss . . .?'

'Miss Perrish,' she said. 'But it's such a frightful name, that you must call me Aunt Cat. It's so much friendlier when we're living in the same house. Don't you agree?'

I couldn't bring myself to speak. I was outraged by her presumption. I wanted Dad to explain to her that Aunt wasn't a name for strangers and paying guests. But, 'How nice of you,' he said, and I was furious with him for failing to protect me from . . . from what?

'Come on, Rosemary,' he said, plucking at my arm. 'We must give Aunt Cat a chance to settle in.'

He had to pluck hard, for I'd almost turned to stone. Afterwards, when he got me up the stairs, he told me never to stare at her like that again because it was rude.

'You're running wild, these days,' he said, looking pretty wild himself with his grey hair sticking out, and his eyes bulging on beanstalks as they did when his temper was about to go. 'You spend too much time alone. Aunt Cat's company is going to be good for you.'

I was frightened of Dad's temper, but I stood my ground. 'I don't need company,' I said. 'I've got Grandpa – and anyway I'm happy on my own!'

Dad's face froze, and I knew I shouldn't have said it like that, as if it didn't matter that Mum had gone. I tried to laugh it off, but I had hurt myself too. The laughter stuck in my throat. Of course I wasn't happy on my own!

I ran upstairs, and slammed the bedroom door. I wanted Dad to follow me, and make up. I wanted him to tell me that our paying guest was just passing through. But he didn't. *He didn't.* I flung myself down upon the windowsill, glaring out at the blue sky, which seemed to mock me with its brightness. The hall clock struck four times. 'There's a stranger in our house, a stranger,' I thought, and the few remaining pillars of my life that hadn't already come down, shook mightily. Not that Dad noticed. Not that he cared.

I roused myself at last. Got out my homework, and did the whole week's worth of it, in a daze and woodenly. By the time Dad called me down for tea, there was nothing left to do.

Reluctantly, I stirred my stiff joints. When I got down, all the best china had been brought out, and a starched tablecloth.

'Aunt Cat will eat with us as it's her first day,' Dad said.

She was at the table already, smelling of scented soap and toothpaste, hair shiny and brushed.

'Is that you, Jane?' Grandpa said, peering at her through milky eyes.

Our paying guest smiled calmly. 'I'm Aunt Cat,' she said, patting Grandpa with her freckled hand. 'I'm living in your lovely basement, and we're going to get on just fine.'

It was a dreadful tea. There were flowers on the table. Flowers indeed! I was desperate to finish eating, and get away from them. When, finally, I did, I went into the front room and switched on the telly, nice and loud.

'Rosemary!' Dad yelled from the dining room. 'Turn that din down, please!'

Smiling with satisfaction, I left it as it was and retired upstairs. I needed time to think. I needed time to be alone. Grandpa knocked on the floor but, for once, I didn't answer him.

Of course, I couldn't sleep that night. Oddly enough, what bothered me more than anything was the thought of Mum's photograph stuffed down the side of the old armchair, with all Miss Perrish's clothes thrown on top of it.

In the end, I got up to make myself my usual cocoa. I left milk in a saucepan on the stove, and peered down the basement stairs. The utility door was closed, but something came over me. I didn't care if I woke our paying guest by creeping in – didn't care what she thought of me. Down I went.

As it turned out, she slept through the squeaking of the door, and even when I passed the bed she never stirred. I found Grandpa's chair, covered with clothes, as I had expected. My fingers probed underneath them.

If she wakes now, I thought grimly, she'll think her new-found niece is a thief. Well, I don't care. All the better, if it drives her away. . . .

The photograph was there. I sighed with relief as if I hadn't expected it to be. Tucking it inside my dressing-gown, I turned to go. Everything in the room was so still – the bed, the figure in it, the shadows upon the wall. Not a sound of life. Not a breath from our sleeping paying guest. It reminded me of Tyger Pool this afternoon, the frozen trees, the mirror-glass lake. . . .

Up in the kitchen, the milk rose in the pan and boiled over noisily. I hurried towards the door, and behind it, in its cage, the bird watched me without blinking.

Silently, I fled.

PART TWO

THE PAYING GUEST

6

Next day was long and difficult. I didn't say a thing at school. I was in a dream. I was in a state of shock. Even afterwards, when Viola dragged me round the shops with a list of baby things for Ellie, I couldn't bring myself to speak.

'What's the matter with you?' Viola said.

I stared at the jars of nappy cream, the bags of cotton wool, the feeding bottles on the shelves, row upon row. Ellie's birth might have taken place a hundred years ago. The thrill of it had faded, leaving me bereft. I should have been so happy, mooching round the shops with my first real friend. But I wasn't.

'You can tell me,' Viola said.

But she was wrong. I couldn't. She paid for the baby things and we ran to catch the bus home. I didn't say a thing until we got off at the Old Guildhall, and nothing lay between me and Aunt Cat. And then, at last, it all poured out. I couldn't help myself.

'We have a paying guest,' I said, desperate to hang onto her, to talk – to do *anything* but go home. 'She's got a funny voice, and all her things

55

are spanking new, and she smiles all the time – I *hate* the way she smiles all the time – and she smells of toothpaste, and scented soap and talcum powder, and she wants me to call her 'Aunt', and she's not my aunt, and she keeps patting me on the arm as if I'm her friend, and I'm not. She's a stranger. I don't know where she comes from, or what she's doing at our house, or why she's come here or anything – and I don't want to. All I want is for her to GO AWAY.'

My voice had risen until I was shouting. My fists were clenched and I was trembling. Viola put a hand on me. I bit my lip to stop myself crying. I must have bitten it very hard, for it started to bleed.

Viola passed me a handkerchief. I felt like a fool, but she smiled at me. 'Look, why don't you come in with me?' she said. 'Forget her for a bit. Come and see how much Ellie's grown. I know it won't make her go away, but you never know.'

She opened the gate but I shook my head. I didn't want to see that Ellie was changing and the world was spinning on. I wanted to stop time – more than stop it. I wanted to put it back.

'Thanks, but no.'

'Oh, come on,' she said, and there was something about the way she said it, as if she really wanted me to. Suddenly, I felt stupid, saying no. Stupid refusing comfort, when I needed it.

I gave her back the handkerchief and followed her through the gate. She led me down the steps and opened the side door. 'Hello, Mum,' she called. 'We're home.'

'Hello, you two,' Mrs Rocket said, as if I were one of the family. The stove was out but she was still smiling. I didn't know how she managed it. In a dressing-gown with a thick jumper over it, she was trying to relight it, surrounded by trays of ash and buckets of coal and a thick pall of smoke. 'You wouldn't hang the nappies out for me?'

We took the bucket of washed nappies and hung them on the line. Ridley was putting his bike in the shed and Mr Rocket, in muddy gardening boots, was pushing Baby Ellie up and down. He had been gardening. He was showing her what he'd done. 'This is soil,' he was saying, tipping up the pram for her to see. 'This is a garden fork. These are primroses. This is the sky . . .'.

We hung out the nappies, and Viola went back in, but I lingered to stare at the fat buds as Mr Rocket named them, the bare ground waiting for its treasures to appear, the robins on the dug earth, the sun behind the trees. Finally, Mr Rocket got round to me. Even me.

'This is *Rose*,' he said, standing in front of me, tilting Ellie so that I could see that she had, indeed, grown. 'You remember, our Rose.'

It was the first time anyone had called me anything but Rosemary, which I hated because Rosemarys were dull, Rosemarys were plain. *Rose*. I liked it. Our Rose. I was glad Viola had asked me in.

'Do you want a cup of tea?' she called, standing by the kitchen door.

We took our tea and cake up to the stage, where Viola did her homework and I helped her, lying on her bed looking up at the huge, dark frame which I had dreamt about. I wondered who had put it there, and how long ago, and why.

Viola finished her homework and packed it away. It was getting dark. She looked down the hall, between the velvet curtains. A slither of moon was shining through a porthole window, high up beneath the roof. She said, 'The owls will be crying in the pines, and the moon will be out over the barn.'

We were bound together by our disappointments. Life not turning out the way it was meant to. I said, 'I'd better go home,' sighing because I couldn't get out of it any more.

'Oh well,' she said.

'I'm glad you invited me.' I managed a smile.

'Any time,' she said, showing me to the door.

'Come again,' her mother called.

I walked home slowly. All the lights were on, right the way down the road. I was nearly at our gate, when a voice summoned me. I looked up. It was Miss Vine.

'Rosemary, a minute of your time!' she called.

I turned onto her path, wondering why she wanted me. But not for long. Her porch light was on, and sitting next to her, surrounded by boxes of seedlings, and plants in pots, was Grandpa. He was wrapped in his big cardigan, cutting up strips of newspaper. Miss Vine had draped a blanket round his shoulders, and her little dog, Frankie, had settled at his feet. They were like two old men together.

'Grandpa?' I said. 'What are you doing here?'

He looked up, but didn't answer me.

'He won't move,' Miss Vine explained. 'He's been here most of the afternoon. Not that I mind, but it's dark now and he'll catch a chill. He's been saying strange things. I can't help worrying.'

I sighed. Grandpa was like a child. I shouldn't have stayed out late. I should have known he'd need me. 'It's time for you to come home now, Grandpa,' I said.

Still he didn't answer. Miss Vine got to her feet. 'Rosemary's come for you,' she said, signalling that I should help her. 'Isn't that nice of her? Now, we're going to take you home between us, so are you ready?'

Together we heaved. Miss Vine was the boniest woman I had ever seen, but there was power in those wiry arms of hers. Grandpa began to move.

'That's it, Grandpa,' I encouraged him. 'Come on.'

He rose to his feet. The blanket fell off him. Frankie nipped out of the way. Bits of newspaper scattered everywhere. We nudged him down Miss Vine's steps onto her front path. Frankie waddled in front of him, as if to say, 'Look, I can do it, so you can too.'

The message seemed to get through. The next thing we knew, he was shaking us off and taking steps on his own. If he had to go home, it wouldn't be on our arms as though he were an invalid!

He made it down the path. We followed him.

'He tells me you have a lodger,' Miss Vine whispered. 'His mind is really wandering. It's such a shame.'

I blushed, and didn't answer. We had reached the road. I opened our gate with 'Habgood. Dog Patrolling, Keep Out' on it, and said, 'Thanks. We can manage from here.' I could see a light in the utility, and the bird cage in the window, behind the blind. I wanted Miss Vine to go away. To think our lodger was a figment of Grandpa's imagination. To never know.

But it was not to be. The front door opened. Aunt Cat came out and stood clearly in a pool of light. 'Rosemary?' she said, in her lilting voice, but with an edge to it which I found irritating. 'Oh, Rosemary, it's you. I was getting worried. And Grandpa too . . .'.

She bustled down the path, an apron over her crisp blouse, and a whiff of perfume coming from her hair.

Miss Vine said, 'I'm afraid he's been sitting next door with me. I hope you don't mind!'

There was an edge to her voice too. Maybe it was because I hadn't admitted that what Grandpa had said was true. Or maybe there was something she didn't like about Aunt Cat. I blushed again. 'Come on, Grandpa,' I urged. I couldn't wait to get inside and shut the door behind us.

Grandpa shuffled up the path. It seemed to take for ever but finally we got him in. Miss Vine departed hurriedly. Aunt Cat shut the door and said, 'What a strange creature she is!'

I found myself bristling. Miss Vine might seem strange if you'd never met her before, but I knew there was more to her than loopy hems and pudding-basin hair. 'She used to be my mum's friend,' I said, loyally. 'She's lived here longer than anyone, except Grandpa.'

'How interesting,' said Aunt Cat. You could tell she wanted to make a good impression on her first day. I glanced around. The house felt warm. I could hear a fire crackling in the front room, and beef sizzling in the pan. 'I'm making us some tea,' she explained. 'I thought I would, seeing as your father cooked for me.'

I couldn't remember the last time we'd had a proper stew instead of sausages and frozen pizzas and frozen chicken pies. But the thought of it didn't please me. Nothing could. 'I'll take Grandpa upstairs until it's ready,' I said, coldly.

'As you wish,' she replied, undeterred. 'But it won't be long.'

Upstairs, I lit the gas and Grandpa sat in front of it. I wouldn't have blamed him if he'd been angry with me for dragging him home. But his mind was on other things.

'She was born just before your mother,' he reminisced. 'I remember it well. Her father was a fierce man. Very private, very proud. Usually away in foreign parts, and the mother had her hands full with them all. Julia was the youngest. Reminds me of her father. It's in the eyes. Do you know, they've all died? How time flies.'

Eventually, Aunt Cat called us for tea. We went down, and Dad was home early from work. I had expected him to mind – even to be cross – about the tea. But he was smiling. *Smiling*! Something

61

had definitely changed in these last few days. I didn't know what to make of it all.

I emptied my plate in silence. When we had finished, Aunt Cat said she wouldn't mind doing it again. She liked to cook. It made no difference whether it was for one or three. I waited for Dad to say that we were managing, but he said 'Thank you', just like that.

I went into the front room. A new plant sat next to the telly. Aunt Cat must have thought that the room needed cheering up. It wasn't very big but it seemed to change everything. It was a reminder of her presence even though she had withdrawn downstairs, shutting the door behind her as if she didn't want to intrude.

I fell asleep in front of the telly and stayed there until there was nothing left to see. I awoke and it was humming, its screen blank. My neck was stiff from the way I'd lain.

Dad came in. He looked surprised to see me there. He was on his way up to bed, his briefcase of work tucked under his arm. 'You should have gone to sleep hours ago,' he said.

'I *have* been asleep,' I said, stretching.

He ruffled the top of my hair. 'Come on, Rosemary,' he said, and up we went. It was a nice moment. I felt close to him.

'Goodnight,' I said, when I reached his door.

He paused. 'I don't want Grandpa going round next door again,' he said. 'We shouldn't bother our neighbours. We can manage on our own. Make sure you get home earlier, Rosemary. It mustn't happen again.' And he went into his room, and shut the door.

7

A noise woke me that night. It was the sound of Aunt Cat's bird which I had jokingly named Pretty Polly, because it was such an ugly thing. I lay listening to it, twice, three times. I would grow used to it in the months to come, but I wasn't used to it yet.

Even when the bird fell silent, I couldn't get back to sleep. My mind raced back and forth over the day. In the darkness, there was no controlling it. Aunt Cat. Miss Vine. Mrs Rocket at her stove. Mr Rocket in the garden. Baby Ellie. Our Rose. Only when it was getting light did my eyelids droop. Dad had to come in and wake me. I went out late and was late for school, arriving after the start of geography.

Viola had saved a place for me – but it was Maple's usual place and she took offence. 'After all I've done for you!' she hissed at Viola, angrily. 'And you'd rather sit with *her*, not me!'

At lunchtime, Ridley came to our table. 'You've really upset Maple,' he said, accusingly. 'How could you be so mean? She thought she was your friend. She's been good to you.'

'Good to me!?' Viola's eyes burned bright. 'If she was *good to me* it was to get to you. And it looks like she's succeeded!'

'You're pathetic sometimes you know,' he said, blushing and hurrying away.

I couldn't help but laugh at him – but it was all right for me. He wasn't my brother. Viola saw it differently. She stared at the table. 'I hate this place,' she said, as if the school were to blame for Maple Cutler. 'He's changed since he's been here. He was the one who used to be *good to me*, but I've lost him now.'

I watched Ridley leaning over Maple's table. Viola was right, about him changing. Once I wouldn't have imagined him with Maple – however hard she tried – or arguing with his sister, the easy smile wiped off his face.

After school, we walked home through Whiteley Wood. Viola couldn't face the sight of Ridley and Maple strolling up the hill. And in any case it was a lovely afternoon. Long shadows stretched under the trees, and the buds seemed to be quivering on the branches as we hurried under them.

Everything was quiet at first, just the rustling trees and us, walking silently. I didn't know what Viola was thinking but I was wondering what Aunt Cat would make for tea. I was thinking I didn't want her wretched meals when, suddenly, I heard shouts ahead.

'What's that?' I said.

'It's coming from Tyger Pool,' Viola said, as an engine grumbled between the trees.

65

We looked at each other. There were more shouts, men's shouts, loud and hard and careless.

'You know what it means?' I said.

'Yes,' she said.

And suddenly, it didn't seem like such a lovely day.

We left the path and pushed through the undergrowth until we were close enough to see for ourselves. Sure enough, the old fence had been replaced by a tall security one. The building work had begun. A row of yellow diggers sat behind the fence, muddy from their first day's activity. A lorry was being piled with ropes and wood and tools, as if the men had done all they could for now, and were going home.

At the sight of them so close to us, we froze. It was as if we'd stumbled on some secret society which would punish us for discovering what it had done – uprooting trees, trampling flowers and grass, even erecting an ugly workman's hut like a poison toadstool beside the pool.

We stared at the pool. The sky might be blue but the water certainly wasn't. Like an angry eye, it seemed to glare at us, and I recalled that time when we had run away, and the other day, when the anger of the pool had seemed to follow me. Why had I returned? The lovely, silver pool I'd enjoyed with Mum, had gone. I should have known better.

I would have turned and gone but Viola caught my arm. 'What's that?' she whispered. 'Look, over there . . .'

I looked, reluctantly. At first I didn't know what

she was on about, but then, between the reeds at the edge of the pool, I saw what she was pronouncing, with horror, to be a dead swan.

'It's only a polythene bag,' I said, dismissively. 'Only a bit of rubbish. Come on . . .'

But she refused to be convinced. We had to wait until the men had climbed into their lorry and gone. Then she went to the fence and followed it until she found a bit where she could clamber through, tearing her clothes.

'Hurry up!' I hissed, as she began to wade among the reeds.

'You're wrong about it being rubbish,' she replied. And there was something about the way she said it.

I didn't want to, but I followed her.

Through the gap in the fence I squeezed, squelching through the reeds to join her. And there it was. Some of its white coat had come off, and its bare patches of flesh were grey. I found a stick and turned it over – not a swan, but Miss Vine's Frankie, waterlogged and dead.

I remember fishing him out of the pool and wrapping him in my coat, explaining to Viola, as I did so, about Miss Vine whose family had died, and only Frankie remained We crept up the stream bed with the bundle pressed against my chest like a guilty secret. I couldn't bring myself to take him up the road for everyone to see. Some things are best hid. When we reached Miss Vine's fence, I looked up at her swaying trees, and said, 'How am I going to tell her?'

I couldn't face it.

'Why don't you come home with me?' said Viola. 'Mum'll find a nice box for him. She'll tell you what to say. She's good at that sort of thing.'

I followed her through the broken fence, imagining Mrs Rocket feeding Ellie, making tea, finding us a box, and all the time smiling serenely. But it can be a disappointing thing, imagining! The sight that greeted us was anything but serene. The garden was full of glass, sheets and sheets of it against the trees, across the path and halfway in, halfway out, of the kitchen door. A filthy Mr Rocket, in overalls, was moving it with the help of a man with sticking-up hair and tattooed hands, whom I'd never seen before. They were shouting at each other. 'Mind that end . . .!' 'Watch it . . .!' 'Down . . .!' 'Stop . . .!' 'A bit to the left . . .!'

'What's going on?' said Viola.

She squeezed through the kitchen door, and I followed her. Sheets of dusty glass had been dumped on Mrs Rocket's bed. I stared at the bed. I don't know why, but a shiver ran through me. Mr Rocket said, 'This is my friend, Mr Eldis. Look what he's found! Isn't he wonderful?'

I looked at Mr Eldis, who was smiling. He had broken teeth and a bent nose. His boots were laced with string. Dad wouldn't have had him in our house, let alone call him *my friend*. And yet. . . .

'Stars for the star-window,' he said, quietly. 'Do you see?'

He tilted a piece of glass, and it sparkled in the light even though it was dusty, and chipped and stained.

'What's it for?' said Viola, unimpressed.

'It's going on the stage,' Mr Rocket said. 'To keep out the draught from the big hall.'

Mrs Rocket snorted. She, too, was unimpressed. She was standing at the sink, flailing nappies so vigorously that foam flew everywhere. 'A *real* day's work,' she said, cheeks bright with indignation, 'would have been to plumb in the washing machine. But, oh no! We can't do anything ordinary like that! We have to find a man who's selling *star-windows*.'

'A man who's giving them,' Mr Rocket said, cheerfully.

'A man who's *giving them*,' she said. Her eyes narrowed to angry slits. Her hands screwed up a soaking nappy and she aimed it at his head.

Mr Rocket ducked. The nappy missed him by an inch, hitting a plate on the dresser. A nice one, edged in gold.

The plate smashed.

Mrs Rocket let out a cry.

'We've got this dead dog,' Viola said, remembering. She dragged me forward with Frankie in my arms. 'We need your help.'

You would have thought the smell would have put them off, but they all gathered round – even Mr Eldis, who touched Frankie with his tattooed hand.

'Poor little thing,' he said in that gentle voice of his.

'Looks like he drowned,' Mr Rocket said.

'We'll find a nice box,' Mrs Rocket said, her anger gone. 'Whose is he?'

I told them all about Miss Vine. Mrs Rocket dug out a scented scarf with multi-coloured spots and sent Mr Rocket for a carved box, which was really much too nice to be buried in the ground, but she said it didn't matter.

We lined the box with the scarf and wedged Frankie in. I closed the lid. Viola made us all a cup of tea and I scrubbed my hands. I wanted to get rid of the musty, rotten smell, but I couldn't – not as long as the box was sitting there, waiting to be taken round.

'Do you want me to come with you?' Mr Rocket volunteered.

I was grateful and relieved. I finished my cup of tea and picked up my coat. It was getting dark outside. I didn't know where the time had gone. Mr Rocket carried the box for me. We passed my house, and went up the path to Forest's Glade. A light shone from the kitchen at the back but everywhere else was dark.

We picked our way over Miss Vine's seedlings. Mr Rocket knocked on the door but there was no response until he knocked again, much louder. Then a light came on in the hall and the outline of a figure moved slowly down it.

The door opened. Miss Vine stood there, not saying anything.

'I'm afraid we've brought your little dog home,'

Mr Rocket said. He held up the box but it was plain that she knew already. Her eyes were sore. She might have been a thousand years old. Her face was broken into blotches of red and pasty grey. Her hair hung lank. Her nose stuck out, white as bone.

'He disappeared last night,' she said, in a wavering voice. 'We went for our bedtime walk as usual and he went – just like that. I called and called but he didn't answer me. In the end, I came back on my own and left the door ajar for him to come in. But he didn't. I stayed up all night but you can feel these things sometimes. I knew he wouldn't. Where was he?'

'In Tyger Pool,' I said, my own voice wavering.

She took the box from Mr Rocket and her hands shook. Her long neck drooped over it. For a moment, her mouth seemed to lose its shape.

'Will you be all right?' Mr Rocket said, touching her arm.

'Of course I will,' she said, drawing back from him, too proud for pity, too private for public sentiment. 'I shall manage, as I always do. Thank you for bringing him home. Goodnight.'

She took the box inside and shut the door.

'Goodnight,' we said.

We were halfway down the path, when Dad's voice came booming over the fence. 'Rosemary!' he called. He sounded furious. 'What time do you call this?'

'Oh, Dad!' I said, remembering what he'd said about being late. 'I'm sorry. Really I am.'

I hurried home, Mr Rocket in tow. Dad stood on the top step, glaring down at us. Mr Rocket said that he could explain, but his friendly ways didn't work this time. Dad dragged me in and slammed the door. He cursed Mr Rocket and Miss Vine. Poor Aunt Cat had been worrying! He'd told me only yesterday! What did I have to say?

Before I could say that the feelings of mere paying guests weren't anything to do with me, the paying guest herself spoke up for me – much to my surprise. Emerging from the kitchen she said, 'I didn't mean to start this. Don't make her come in at a special time on account of me.' And she smiled, as if she wanted, more than anything, to be my friend. 'Let her have her tea,' she pleaded. 'I've kept it on a plate.'

The words pacified Dad, just like that. He let me take my tea into the dining room, where his work was spread out on the table. I sat at the end, trying to keep out of his way. It was a fitting finish to a dreadful day. We didn't speak until I'd eaten. I rose to go next door and drown myself in telly, and he said, 'What were you doing round at Miss Vine's again?' He didn't even look up.

It was a waste of time explaining. He wouldn't care. 'Nothing you'd be interested in,' I said.

8

When I went up to bed that night, Grandpa was standing before the bathroom mirror, his face covered with soap, staring at his eyes which were the only bit of him that he could see. I leaned against the door frame, but he didn't notice me, just kept staring.

'What is it, Grandpa?' I said.

He didn't turn his head. Didn't even say anything. Gently, I washed the soap away and led him back to his room. It was in chaos. Newspapers and scrapbooks were scattered everywhere.

'What's going on, Grandpa?' I said.

Again he didn't answer me. Just stared at the newspapers, stared and stared, as if he was looking for something, back there in his past, which had disappeared.

I blamed myself, for leaving Grandpa with Aunt Cat. Her presence had unsettled him. I made a point of coming straight home from school, after that, even resisting Viola's invitations to tea. Grandpa wasn't crashing about in the night any more but he was always up in his room, shuffling his old newspapers around as if they contained some sort of secret key, if only he could find it.

Maybe he was looking for the boy he used to be again, in a world that was spinning on so fast that it was frightening. Flowers were bursting out as if they couldn't wait, and it was only April, but the nights were so warm. I would sit at the open bedroom window, listening to Pretty Polly squawking in the dining room, where Aunt Cat sometimes brought him for a change of scenery.

I would listen to the murmur of her talking to him, and the traffic which rumbled until the early hours of the morning, and the noises of the wood. I had always thought the wood was silent in the night. But I was discovering it wasn't. I could hear things. It was as if it, too, was murmuring.

'They've started draining Tyger Pool,' Dad said one morning, throwing aside the newspaper.

Aunt Cat put down his breakfast. Gone were the days of cornflakes and bits of toast. Not only did she cook tea, but she now brought the smell of bacon and sausages to the furthest corners of our house.

I didn't know what had happened to Dad's pride and independence. Mrs Cutler wouldn't have allowed her paying guests to bustle about her house as if they owned it. Mrs Cutler, I was sure, kept her paying guests in place!

But then, Mrs Cutler's paying guests were proper paying guests. They were either tourists or businessmen. They had places to go to, and things to do. They weren't like Aunt Cat who went out every day but didn't seem to be on holiday, or going to work, or to visit friends.

'Don't you wonder where she comes from,' Viola said, 'and what she's doing here? Don't you wonder where she goes, every day?'

I wouldn't answer her. Maybe I knew instinctively that it was better not to find out. All I knew was that every morning she went out dressed in clothes which looked as if they had just been removed from the Cellophane, and every afternoon she was back again. I tried to tell myself that I didn't care what her business was, or where she went.

'She's done wonders with Grandpa,' Dad said. 'He's more like his old self than he's been all year.'

'Just because Grandpa's quiet,' I said, 'it doesn't mean that everything's all right.'

He didn't answer me, just rushed off to work, slamming the door behind him. I lingered at the breakfast table. My time was my own. The Easter holidays had begun. Aunt Cat had gone out. Grandpa and I were alone.

Alone. I savoured it, walking through the house from room to room. I was free. Free to do anything.

Maybe it was Pretty Polly's shriek that made me think of going downstairs. Or maybe I did want to find out about Aunt Cat, after all. I opened the utility door, and went in. Everything was tidy and clean. A row of plants sat on the windowsill. Light shone between their leaves, casting the whole room green.

I began to explore, turning things over, opening drawers, even looking under the bed – goodness knows what for. All the while, Pretty Polly watched me. I couldn't believe what he was turning into, with his long, striped feathers and shiny claws. I couldn't believe how much he had grown. It was as if the coming of spring had affected him, too. Only his eyes were the same, black and watchful.

Grandpa called me, and I was glad to get away from their pitiless glare. He wanted his jacket, he was going into town, would I come with him? I left the room, shutting the door carefully behind me. I had found nothing. No past, no secrets, no tell-tale clues as to what Aunt Cat was really like behind her newly-minted look, and bright smile.

We caught a bus outside the Old Guildhall. I worried that town might be too much for Grandpa but he seemed to savour his freedom, as much as I did. We spent the morning buying a book for me, and a new pipe for him. I reminded him that he didn't smoke any more, but he wanted it all the same. We dropped into George's Take-Away on the way home, and bought bags of fish and chips which we ate in the back garden in the sunshine.

I pretended I couldn't hear the distant machinery in Whiteley Wood. Grandpa admired his new pipe, turning it over in his hands lovingly. He began to browse through my book, but tiredness caught up with him. He wandered indoors and fell asleep on the settee.

I covered him lightly, pulling the curtains behind him to protect him from the sun. He would sleep for hours, I could tell. I went out, shutting the door behind. My time was now my own. I would treat myself and go round to Viola's.

Like a spring lamb, I skipped down the garden and over the fence, sliding between trees on which new leaves hung like pieces of fresh silk. Through Viola's fence I climbed. Rows of vegetables had sprung up in Mr Rocket's garden. Everything had changed in just a few weeks. I tried to open the side door but it seemed to be stuck. A voice called, 'The hinges have snapped! The door's wedged so you'll have to climb through the window!' It was Viola.

She clattered up the steps into the kitchen, laughing at my expression of surprise. When she reached out to open the window, the whole thing crashed down. She laughed again. 'The sash has broken too,' she said, pulling aside the curtains to make way for me. 'But never mind that. Come in.'

I clambered in. 'It's so good to see you,' she exclaimed. 'And what a day you've chosen for it. Come and see what we've done!'

Her hair was white with paint. Her face was smudged with dust. I followed her down the steps into the room underneath the stage. It had been transformed. White paint covered the stone walls and a hole had been knocked through the outer wall, to let in the light. A small window frame had been inserted and covered with polythene. The floor had been scrubbed and was carpeted with a bright rug. The doors at the end were open and furniture was being brought down from the big hall.

'What do you think?' said Viola. She sounded, for the first time, as if she didn't hate the place.

'I think it's *beautiful*!' I said, staring at the shining floor which had never seen sunlight before. 'What can I do to help?'

Mrs Rocket staggered beneath her end of an ancient radiogram which Mr Rocket was pulling down the steps, and Ridley – in his yellow, holey sweater, and smiling like the boy he used to be – was steering. She said, 'I could do with someone at this end. It weighs a ton.'

I helped them, and they wove their spell on me again. The spell of being 'one of the family'. The magic of belonging. After the radiogram, we brought down a huge mirror in a gilt frame, and a painting of an apple and a small toy, and a piano with brass candle holders, and a bookcase. Together we set sofas and an armchair around a new fireplace, built of stone. We put a table in front of the polythene window, with a plate of scented rose petals on it, and an old telly.

When, finally, we stopped, none of us could believe our eyes. The place beneath the stage had turned into such a cosy living room that it might have been inhabited for years.

'Look what we've achieved since you started throwing nappies at me!' Mr Rocket teased.

Mrs Rocket laughed and said. 'Perhaps it was worth breaking that plate, after all! Now then, it's time to eat.'

The Rockets, I was learning, never missed the chance to celebrate. Mrs Rocket brought down an inaugural tea of sausage rolls and mountains of

78

sandwiches made with home-baked bread, scones with jam and cream and a cake covered in icing which was crisp on top, but when Viola stuck her finger in it, was as soft as marshmallow inside.

'Really, Viola!' her mother said, putting down a stack of plates. 'Ridley, the kettle's boiling. Make us a pot of tea. Rose, go upstairs and call Mr Eldis . . .'

I didn't know what she was on about. Mr Eldis? Upstairs? She saw my hesitation, and pointed to the corner of the room. 'Up there,' she explained, on her way back to the kitchen.

I opened what I had thought was a cupboard door. To my surprise, a staircase wound up into the dark. I climbed it, savouring the aroma of sweet wood, and came out through another door onto the stage. The velvet curtains had been taken down and a scaffold erected, upon which Mr Eldis stood, puttying. He had turned the huge, arched frame into a window. From one side of the stage to the other and right up to the roof, its criss-cross bars were full of sparkling glass.

I couldn't take my eyes off the glass. There was no sun in the hall but it still shone like a thousand jewels, or as if it had its own light.

'It's time for tea,' I said.

Mr Eldis leapt from the scaffold. 'Thank goodness for that,' he exclaimed. 'I could eat a horse!' and he bounded down the stairs, leaving me behind.

I was hungry too but I didn't follow him. I was mesmerized. The closer I looked at the glass, the more it shone. It shimmered as if it was made of sequins, or sunlight on a moving sea, or. . . . What had Mr Eldis called the glass, that first day? *Stars for the star-window.*

'Are you coming, Rose?' Mrs Rocket called.

It broke the spell – which was just as well. I hurried downstairs and everyone was piling their plates with food. The candles had been lit on the piano. I was missing the fun. Missing the chance to eat myself silly and laugh myself – as indeed I did – into a idiotic state.

When we had cleared most of the plates, and the jokes had run dry, Ridley opened the radiogram and put on records, one after another. We began to fool around. We began to dance. Even me.

Mrs Rocket waltzed like a ballroom artiste with Baby Ellie in her arms. Ridley clapped his hands and did Mick Jagger leaps. Mr Rocket swayed to his own beat. Viola and I pretended we were ballerinas on a stage.

This is me, I thought. Me dancing. Me with them. Me, *Rose*. Not Rosemary. Not her.

Viola pirouetted around me, and Mr Eldis waltzed me lightly, despite his boots! Mrs Rocket let me dance with Ellie until she began to cry. And Ridley – fantastic Ridley – twizzled me round and round, holding me tight.

They were as much family to me, in those minutes, as anyone had been. They were. I swear it.

But nothing lasts for ever.

'*So, this is where you are!*' Maple Cutler said.

We all span round. She had plucked back a corner of the polythene, and was peering in on us. 'I knocked and knocked,' she said to Ridley as if the rest of us weren't there. 'I thought you and I were going out tonight?!'

Ridley stared, horrified. 'Oh Maple!' he said. 'I'm sorry. I forgot!'

'So I see,' she said, looking daggers at me.

He let go of my hands, as if they were poisoned. 'I'll go and get ready,' he said. 'I won't be long.'

The record came to an end. There was an awkward silence.

'Why don't you come in?' Mrs Rocket said, pulling down the rest of the polythene.

Maple clambered through the opening and sidled round the table with the remnants of tea on it.

'Have a piece of cake while you're waiting,' Mrs Rocket said.

But Maple looked at it disdainfully. She couldn't see what a lovely cake it was, or what a beautiful table it sat upon, or in what a lovely room.

Ridley returned, hair smoothed down, in a clean jumper. 'Let's go, shall we?' he said.

Maple followed him out. Mrs Rocket tacked back the polythene, saying that if Mr Rocket didn't mend the kitchen door, they'd have everybody coming in and out this way. The party felt well-and-truly over. Maple's complaints faded into the distance.

'I remember *my* "Maple Cutler",' Mr Rocket teased. 'Bleached-out lips, black eyes, back-combed hair. . . .'

Mrs Rocket laughed at him. 'Was that really me?'

81

'Of course it was!' Mr Rocket said. 'You were quite a sight, believe me!'

Mrs Rocket smiled gently. 'Poor Maple,' she said. 'I don't think she knows what to make of us. . . .'

Their voices droned on. They drifted up to the kitchen, and I could have followed them. Viola was collecting plates. I could have helped her do the dishes. But I didn't. I returned upstairs where Mr Eldis was packing away his things.

I watched him moving quietly, wondering that I hadn't noticed him before, in our town where nobody was a total stranger. He looked up, and smiled at me. It was getting dark outside. 'See you again,' he said and off he went.

Suddenly I realized how late it was, and a stab of guilt went through me. I flung myself down on the nearest bed. I had abandoned Grandpa again. He would have woken to find me gone, with no message or anything.

I should have returned, there and then. But it was the strangest thing. The window seemed to *hold* me. Not just yet, I thought, lying back against a pillow, and peering through it at the furniture in the big hall. The stage was warm. Even the hall seemed to be cast in a faint glow. It reminded me of early mornings in Whiteley Wood, with beams of sunlight penetrating between trees and mist.

I found myself drifting into a middle-land between wakefulness and sleep. Into the place where dreams begin. I floated through the mist, and who I was, and where I should have been meant nothing any more. The mist glittered as if made of frost, or pricking stars. I reached the window – and the hall had gone. Real trees, not furniture, spread out in front of me. I was at some sort of *boundary*. Beyond it lay Whiteley Wood, and Tyger Pool.

But it was a Tyger Pool I'd never seen before, its water bubbling like an unattended stew. I pressed my face against the glass. Out of the pool, something was emerging. Black feathers, yellow feathers, red talons, red beak. I watched the creature rise. I saw it all.

And it saw me.

Nothing in my perfect day had prepared me for this. The creature's wings unravelled right across the pool. I couldn't imagine them contracting to the span of a mere cage. But for all that, it was Pretty Polly, unmistakably! I recognized the eyes. They were fixed on me. As if I were the enemy.

I had felt safe behind the glass, but suddenly I was terrified. The creature beat its wings and rose, slowly. Its eyes never left my face as it came for me, with talons outstretched. . . .

9

I awoke. A whole night had passed, and it was morning. I was still wearing yesterday's clothes but the bedcovers had been pulled over me. Viola slept in the spare bed at my side.

I lay looking at the sun shining upon the furniture in the big hall. Soon it would reach the new window, Mr Eldis's star-window, which was sparkling already. Not that I cared what it looked like any more. For I had other things on my mind. I was going insane.

Who but a mad girl, I asked myself, would have dreamt what I had, and then awoken, terrified that it hadn't been a dream – that it had all been true? And who but a mad girl would have dreamt such a strange thing, anyway? I was letting my grief and anger run away with me!

I lay, overwhelmed with shame, marvelling at my capacity for hating anything connected with poor Aunt Cat, who had been kind. It wasn't her fault that I couldn't stand her smile, or her friendly ways. She'd thought that she was helping when she'd started making breakfast, making tea, buying plants for the front room, doing jobs around the house.

Round and round my thoughts whirled. When I got up, there was only one thing certain on my mind.

I would be nice to Aunt Cat.

Then I wouldn't, ever, dream such a thing again.

I went home that morning, bracing myself for trouble because I had been out all night. But Dad had gone to work and Aunt Cat, in her nightdress, said, 'Have you eaten? Shall I get you something?' as if there was nothing to worry about. Before I could answer, she had lain strips of bacon in the pan, humming a little tune to herself.

'I'm sorry about last night,' I said. 'I was over at the Old Guildhall.'

'We know you were,' she said. 'Mr Rocket called.'

'Is Dad angry with me?' I asked. It was a stupid question. He was bound to be.

She turned the bacon in the pan, didn't even look at me. Her hum had turned into a purr. It was the funniest thing. 'There's no need to worry,' she said. 'I smoothed him down.'

I tried to feel grateful. Really I did. 'I could finish that,' I offered, 'if you want to go out.'

'I thought I wouldn't. Not today,' she said, deftly flipping the bacon onto a plate. 'I thought I'd take a little holiday.'

'Oh, that's nice,' I said, trying to sound sincere. For the next few days, I smiled and said that everything was nice, from the taking down of the hems of my school summer dresses, to the chocolate rabbit Aunt Cat gave me on Easter Day. In the end, I couldn't switch off the wretched smile. It was stuck, like sunlight drowning in quick-set concrete.

Not that Aunt Cat was entirely to blame. I had been dreading Easter anyway. Like Christmas, it contained memories, and the worst of them was going to the Town Hall on Easter Sunday night, for the concert which had been Mum's big treat of the year. However quickly the tickets sold, we had never missed it.

And this year we were going, as usual. Dad had managed to get tickets – although I didn't know why. It hung over me for days. By the time Easter Day arrived, I could hardly think of anything else. Miss Vine called with a chocolate egg and I thanked her for it, miserably. She stood on the front step, but Dad didn't invite her in as he had done on Christmas Day.

'Come and see my garden, sometime,' she said to me, as she turned away.

I was surprised by the invitation. Miss Vine might have been my mother's friend, but she had guarded her privacy, all the same. I couldn't ever remember being invited round before.

'Lunch is ready,' Aunt Cat called, before I could answer.

Dad shut the front door. We sat down to eat and I was a million miles away. I smiled and said that the lunch, the weather, the newly-mown lawn outside the window – all of it was nice. Smiled and nodded, smiled and nodded, but the real me was locked up inside, nursing her growing dread.

Only later, when Mrs Cutler phoned, did my feelings change. Were we all right, she wanted to know? Would we come for drinks this evening? Dad took the phone from me and said that we were fine and going out, so firmly that it heartened me. It came to me that Mum might have gone, but we were still a family. Dad, and Grandpa, and me. Perhaps that was why he'd bought the tickets. For us to be together. Perhaps the concert would be all right, after all.

I hurried upstairs to dress. I hadn't wanted to before, and now I did. I stood before the dressing-table mirror in the new clothes we'd bought because I'd grown. I was a different girl to the one I'd been last year. Dad wouldn't notice – he saw me every day – but if Mum had returned. . . .

I smoothed down the dress. It had a velvet top, with long sleeves, and a tartan skirt. I felt nice in it, with my brushed hair curling under for once, the way I always wanted it to.

'Rosemary!' Dad called. 'It's time to go.'

I gave myself a last glance in the mirror. Even I could see that I was getting to look more like Mum. 'We haven't forgotten you,' I said, addressing the figure in the mirror as if she were Mum. 'This evening's just for you. Do you like the dress? Silly question – I know you do. . . .'

'Rosemary!' Dad called again.

I hurried downstairs. Dad, in best suit and new tie, was carrying Grandpa's supper on a tray into the front room, where Grandpa watched the telly in his old cardigan.

'What's going on?' I said. 'Where's Grandpa's waistcoat? Why isn't he dressed?'

'Grandpa's not coming,' Dad said. 'He isn't up to it.'

'Isn't up to it?' I said, my sense of dread returning.

Grandpa didn't as much as move his head. 'He doesn't want to,' Dad said.

'Then I shall stay with him,' I said. My voice was shaking.

'Don't be ridiculous,' Dad said. 'We're going to be late. Come on.'

He was right – or so I told myself. I was being ridiculous. Here was my chance to have him to myself, and I was making a fuss as if I didn't want to! I gave Grandpa a big hug, promising to bring him back a programme, and followed Dad out into the hall.

And there stood Aunt Cat, resplendent in an evening dress, carrying an embroidered silk shawl!

'Good, we're ready,' Dad said, opening the front door, car keys jangling in his hand. Aunt Cat moved towards it.

'I don't understand,' I said.

'Understand what?' Dad said.

They both turned to look at me.

'Are we dropping Aunt Cat off somewhere?' I asked.

Dad laughed as if what I'd said was funny. 'Don't be silly, Rosemary,' he said. 'We can't waste Grandpa's ticket. Aunt Cat's coming instead.'

I stood there, trembling with shock and rage and sheer disbelief. I remember it all so clearly. That sense of having been outwitted. Of having been betrayed. I looked at my dad, who didn't want to spend an evening with me, after all. My dad who didn't want me. 'We can't leave Grandpa on his own,' I said coldly. 'Never mind me. You two go.'

Dad's temper flared, as if he'd had enough of me. 'You're making an exhibition of yourself!' he said, shortly. 'Get in the car!'

I slunk into the car, ashamed of myself for not making a stand, but if Dad had said another word, I would have dissolved into tears – and I couldn't do that in front of Aunt Cat. Dad slammed the front door, and hurried down the steps. An almighty squawk arose from the utility, as he passed its window.

'Someone doesn't like you going out,' he joked with Aunt Cat.

'Someone doesn't like sharing me!' she said, in that lilting voice of hers.

They were still laughing at the funny ways of pets when we reached the centre of town. Dad couldn't find a parking place and had to drive round and round. I was delighted to see the laugh wiped off his face. He prided himself on never being late.

We hurried up the Town Hall steps, Dad apologizing because the concert had begun. It was only when we sank into our seats, that my thoughts returned to Mum. I hadn't realized how strongly her presence would have lingered here. It was *everywhere.* In *everything.*

The Town Hall was lovely in those days. They've pulled it down since then, and built a new one with the best acoustics for miles around. But the old one had velvet seats and gold trims, and private boxes with cherubim holding lamps that dimmed.

I closed my eyes to shut out Aunt Cat. I had to remind myself that, whatever Dad had turned it into, this concert was my memorial to Mum. '*I know that my Redeemer liveth,*' the soprano sang in her clear voice, which rose to the very top of the Town Hall, not to say anything of the dark place inside my heart, where my loss hurt most of all. '*And that he shall stand . . . at the latter day . . . upon the earth. . . .* '

The words shone like bright stars watching over me. Like new spring life. They told me that there was hope even though my eyes were closed, and I was stuck in the dark by Aunt Cat's side, and Dad had forgotten, and Grandpa was fading away.

Only when the lights went up and the clapping began, did I open my eyes. Aunt Cat was waving her programme. 'That was lovely!' she exclaimed. But if she'd known how lovely it really was, she wouldn't have said anything – she'd have savoured it as I did, deep inside.

Dad got up briskly. He began pushing us towards the aisle, muttering about getting out before the crush. But I knew it wasn't that. I knew that he had been affected too. He took my arm and steered me outside. When we got there, the stars were shining.

Dad and I stood together, drawn close to each other.

Aunt Cat flung her shawl around her shoulders, and said, 'Do you know, I think there's a hint of frost on the ground?'

It broke the spell. 'Here, let me . . .' Dad said, moving away from me, to help her adjust her shawl.

I turned towards the street where we'd left the car. But Dad called me back. 'Not that way, Rosemary,' he said. 'The night is young. We're going for a meal!'

I looked at the restaurants and pubs around Town Square. 'Whatever for?' I said. 'We ate at teatime.'

Dad tried to take my arm, but I wouldn't let him. 'Look,' he said. 'How about over there?'

He pointed to a restaurant with empty tables overlooking the floodlit square. 'Looks good to me,' Aunt Cat said, enthusiastically.

Dad led us into the restaurant. What we ate, I can't remember. I picked at my food and watched people going up and down outside. First a noisy, drunken crowd I recognized from school, then a tramp scavenging through bins, then the surge after the cinema. When they had finished eating, Dad and Aunt Cat talked and talked. I didn't listen to them. I was too busy longing for the day to be over. Too busy longing to go home – although Dad and Aunt Cat were in no hurry. . . .

We stayed until only the tramp was left, lying on a bench. We could even hear him snoring when we came out.

'I don't know what this town is coming to!' Dad said. 'Scavengers and drunken children. It never used to be like this.'

We passed the bench on the way to the car. Dad and Aunt Cat were ahead. They didn't seem to notice me trailing behind. I came level with the bench, and the tramp stopped snoring. He raised his head and looked me straight in the eye. I recognized him. He was Mr Eldis!

'Hello, Rosemary,' he greeted me.

In the artificial light, his eyes were the brightest, most probing blue.

'Hello,' I said, uncertainly.

'I should have known we'd meet,' he said, sitting up and fumbling in the pocket of his old coat. 'Here. I've got something for you. . . .'

He held out his hand, but I backed away. It was ridiculous. I had even danced with him. But I couldn't help myself.

'It's all right,' he said. 'Here. Don't be afraid.'

I hesitated.

'Rosemary!' Dad called.

'Take it,' Mr Eldis said.

Half of me was full of questions, but the other half was relieved to get away. When I caught up with Dad he said that I should never talk to strangers. He could have been drunk. He could have been dangerous. I didn't try explaining that he was Mr Rocket's friend.

We climbed into the car, but it was only when we were driving through the streets, light splashing through the windows, that I looked at what Mr Eldis had given me. He must have got it out of a bin. It was one of those paperweights that snow when shaken. It was dented, but I could still see that it contained a little scene – houses, a spire, a dark blue night. The snow was made of silver, which sparkled as it fell out of the sky.

I'll give it to Grandpa, I decided. The dent was only small, and he could put it on his desk, to keep his papers from scattering.

When we arrived home, the house was dark and silent. There were no shrieks from the utility, much to my relief, nor was the telly still on. Grandpa must have gone up to bed early. His tray of supper lay untouched. The front room looked immaculate, the settee undisturbed as if he'd hardly sat on it.

'Thank you for a wonderrful evening,' purred Aunt Cat, yawning, and stretching herself.

'We'll do it again,' Dad said, as she went down the basement stairs.

I was tired, too. I said goodnight to Dad, and went up to bed. But, passing Grandpa's room, I decided to go in. Maybe he was still awake. I could give him the paperweight. I could talk to him.

I crossed to his desk, and switched on the lamp. And in the sudden light, I couldn't believe my eyes. I let out a cry. Grandpa's bed was as untouched as the settee downstairs – but it was all that was! His wardrobe door hung open, and half his clothes had been pulled out. Old shoes littered the floor. Even ornaments which had stood on his shelves for years lay smashed on the ground.

It was as if Grandpa had had a brainstorm. I stood, transfixed. I didn't know what to do. Dad came rushing into the room. He let out a cry too. He ran out of the room, calling Grandpa's name. Aunt Cat appeared in her nightdress. I turned away from her, instinctively. I plunged into Grandpa's wardrobe where his suitcase had gone. So had his overcoat, and best waistcoat and cardigan. . . .

'This is what I get for going out and leaving him!' I cried, rifling through the few clothes that remained. 'I should have stayed, like I wanted to. *Grandpa's gone!*'

10

Aunt Cat took over. She was the one who kept her head while Dad went into a frenzy, and I was too stunned to know what to do. She phoned the hospital and the police. She searched all the front gardens down our road, knocking on Miss Vine's door although the house was dark, and there was no sign of life. Still in her nightdress, with only her silk shawl thrown over it, she went into Whiteley Wood, and even up the main road to Emmanuel, to see if Grandpa was at Mum's graveside.

'It's going to be all right,' she promised, when she came back, empty-handed. 'The police will find him. He's an old man. He can't have gone far.'

I'd been saying it for an hour, but Dad believed her, not me. She persuaded him to sit by the fire in the front room, and drink a cup of sweet tea. 'Perhaps you had better go to bed,' she said to me. 'There's no point in all of us going without sleep. Hopefully, he'll be back when you wake up in the morning.'

I would have stayed if Dad had wanted me. I would have sat beside him on the settee and held his hand all night, but instead I trailed up to bed alone and cried alone, my imagination conjuring up dreadful things until I couldn't stand it any more.

I got out of bed and pulled back the curtains. To my relief, there were streaks of morning in the sky. I dressed and went out. The front-room light was still on. I passed it without looking in. There was one place I had to go, even if Aunt Cat had been to it already. I felt the magnet-pull of Tyger Pool.

I had been fighting it all night, and I couldn't fight any more. Down to Whiteley Wood I hurried – over our fence, into the stream bed, down and down as if, again, I had a secret which nobody must discover. It was as if I knew, just knew, that Grandpa would be in the water, bobbing among the reeds like Miss Vine's Frankie had been.

My heart was hammering. I pushed myself on until I reached the building site. And in the grey, first light, I saw trenches, diggers hanging over them waiting for the morning when the work would resume. More trees were down. Piles of chain-sawed logs were stacked beside a track which had been gouged out of the wounded ground in which they'd grown.

I reached the metal fence and peered through. At first I couldn't make out what I was looking at, in the grey light. Couldn't take it in. But then I realized.

Relief washed over me. I had got it wrong about the pool calling me, and I had got it wrong about Grandpa's dreadful end. The only dreadful end was Tyger Pool's own. It had gone, its water drained away, its empty shell filled with gravel and rocks.

I should have wept, but I laughed instead. Laughed with relief because Grandpa hadn't drowned. I called his name, and it echoed round the wood, but he didn't answer me.

I turned and set out for home. It had begun to rain, the first rain for weeks. I passed the War Memorial, and started up our road. A few curtains had been drawn back, but it was too early for the milkman to have called. I got as far as Miss Vine's gate, which was open though she usually kept it closed. I stared at the carved words, Forest's Glade. And suddenly I *really* knew where Grandpa had gone. She mightn't hear Aunt Cat's knock. But she would hear mine. . . .

I ran up the path, and hammered on the door. 'Miss Vine!' I called. 'It's me! Rosemary!'

It was as if she'd been waiting for me. I didn't need to say, 'Is Grandpa with you?' She opened up and said, 'Come inside,' almost hauling me in, and shutting the door behind us. 'Your grandpa's upstairs in my room,' she said. 'Come into the kitchen. I'm making him some breakfast. You can take it up to him.'

She led me down a cold, bare hall into a kitchen with a concrete floor and the sort of china sink that I didn't realize people had in their houses any more. There were no pictures on the walls, no pretty things. No hints of Miss Vine's past, or memories of her family. A mop and pail in a corner.

An empty dog basket on the floor. A smell of carbolic soap, a window ledge full of cuttings.

'I'm making scrambled eggs,' Miss Vine said, pouring the mixture into a pan on a prehistoric gas stove, and scraping the stuff around until it was cooked enough to pile onto a plate.

'What's he doing here?' I asked. 'We've been looking for him everywhere. Why did he come to you? What happened to him?'

'I wish I knew,' she said. 'He woke me with his knocking. He was in a dreadful state. He said that I wasn't to tell anyone where he was. What could I do? There were no lights next door. I thought you were all asleep. I put him to bed and sat over him. It seemed like the easiest thing. I hoped you wouldn't know he'd gone until morning. He's tossed and turned and cried all night, but he still won't tell me what's wrong. Just keeps on saying he won't go home.'

I took the tray with the eggs on it. Surely he would tell *me*.

'You'll see the light under the door,' Miss Vine said.

Up I went. There were no carpets on the stairs, and the oldest wallpaper I had ever seen hung on the walls. Forest's Glade might look like a grand house from the road, but it wasn't grand inside – at least not any more. I reached a dark landing. Under one of the doors, I saw a strip of light. 'Grandpa,' I whispered. 'Don't be frightened. It's only me.'

I opened the door and crept in. Grandpa lay asleep, a tiny figure in what must have been the biggest bed in the whole world. Nothing in the rest of the house had prepared me for it. A gilded counterpane lay over him, made of the same red stuff as the canopy over his head, and the curtains which hung on either side, tied back by silk cords. The wooden panels on the bed had been carved with flowers, embossed with bright strips of metal and pieces of ivory. By it stood a gilded chair. Upon the wall hung a sabre, and a photograph of a proud, military man, and a thin wife who looked like Miss Vine, but of another generation. Upon the floor stood what had once been a sumptuous Indian rug, though it was now worn.

I put the tray down on a bedside table, which had legs carved to look like elephants. The thought of thin Miss Vine owning this exotic bed – no doubt brought back by her father from some distant place – struck me with awe. It also made me want to laugh so much that I had to bite my lip. And even then I laughed. I couldn't help myself.

Grandpa opened his eyes. He didn't say, as he so often did at home, 'Where am I?' He just stared at me. I sat on the gilded chair – nervously, as if I was afraid I'd break it – and fed him the scrambled eggs.

He ate them meekly, without a word of protest. It was hard to believe that this was the same rampaging man who'd turned his bedroom into such a mess. The man who, despite his age, had packed his bag and run away. When he had finished, I put aside the plate. 'What happened, Grandpa?' I asked him.

He closed his eyes, as if he didn't want to remember. 'The bird,' he whispered. I could hardly hear him. I made him say it again. 'It was the bird,' he said.

'The bird?' I said, and I went cold inside.

'That squawking, nasty thing,' he said, shivering. 'You know who I mean. He attacked me.'

I did indeed know who he meant. Pretty Polly, who I had always hated, right from the start. But he couldn't have attacked Grandpa.

'You've got it wrong,' I said. 'He's in a cage. You must have had a bad dream.'

Grandpa opened his eyes and looked at me, as if I were a prize fool. He removed his hands from the warm bed, and held them out to me. *See*, the gesture said. They were covered with red scratches, which had bled and dried. What with the swelling and the bruising, they looked like a pair of ripe plums.

I stared at them, astonished. '*He attacked me!*' Grandpa repeated, leaning forward to make sure I understood. And where his head had been, blood stained the pillow.

And then I knew, without a shadow of doubt, that Aunt Cat's Pretty Polly had smashed Grandpa's ornaments, turned his whole room upside down, got out of his cage, somehow, and attacked him. I remembered my dream. It had been a warning!

Miss Vine knocked on the door, and poked her head around it. 'I've brought you up some tea.'

'Come and see this,' I said, my voice shaking with anger and fear. For what monster of a pet did

Aunt Cat keep in the utility? And what else could it do?

She crossed the room, and looked at Grandpa's hands. I showed her the pillow. 'You must get your father, Rosemary,' she said. 'He's got to see this for himself.'

Grandpa protested, but Miss Vine was right. Dad had to be told. And not just about Pretty Polly, but that Grandpa had been found.

I hurried home and pounded on the front door. Dad answered it. His hair was tousled. He still wore last night's suit, but it was so crumpled that it didn't look like a best suit any more.

'Dad,' I cried, clutching him. 'Grandpa's next door. Miss Vine's got him. Dad, you've got to come and see.'

'See what?' Dad said, only half-awake.

I tried to tug him out of the house, but Aunt Cat emerged from the front room, looking tousled too. 'This is all your fault!' I burst out, before she could say anything. 'Your fault, and that bloody bird of yours!'

'Rosemary!' Dad cried. He sounded shocked, but at least I'd woken him.

I told him what had happened. It all poured out. Aunt Cat didn't interrupt me, but there was something in her face that I'd never seen before, but had suspected, all along. Something that wasn't gentle and sweet, and didn't want to be friends with me. Something very far from kind. I have never forgotten it, in all this time.

'I keep him in his cage,' she said, when I had finished. 'It's always locked. He couldn't have got out. Miss Vine must have planted the idea in Grandpa's head. You know how confused he gets. It could easily be done, and she doesn't like me. I can tell.'

'Doesn't she?' Dad said, grimly. 'Rosemary, you come with me. You and I are going to sort this out! Cat, you stay here. It won't take long.'

It didn't take long. Dad beat upon Miss Vine's door, shouting her name for all the road to hear. But when he saw Grandpa's wounds, his anger drained away.

'What sort of bird would do a thing like this?' he said, shaking his head.

'That's what we'd all like to know,' Miss Vine said, quietly washing Grandpa's hands, dabbing them with ointment, wrapping them in bandages.

'It'll have to go,' Dad said. 'There are no two ways about it. We shall have to tell Aunt Cat.'

There was no need, however. When we got home, the bird had flown. Literally. Aunt Cat, with tears running down her face, said that she had freed it, just in case. She shouldn't have kept a wild bird in a cage. She had done wrong. She wanted to tell Grandpa that it was safe to come home. She wanted to apologise for her part in driving him away.

It was the first time I'd seen Aunt Cat cry. The first time she'd shown any sort of feeling, other than to smile. And all for a wretched, black-eyed, red-clawed, nasty-tempered bird! So distraught was she that Dad had to put his arms around her, to calm her down. She cried upon his shoulder and I had to walk away.

I went up to Grandpa's room, which I cleared from top to bottom, placing Mr Eldis's snow-scene on the desk, to replace a broken ornament. Dad came in. He looked exhausted, stretched out thin. 'You've done a grand job, Rosemary,' he said, looking around. 'If the room's ready, we could go and get Grandpa back.'

We found him downstairs in Miss Vine's kitchen. The back door was open. He was sitting, watching the rain. Dad told Miss Vine that Pretty Polly had gone. She slipped away discreetly – as if it were our business, not hers, to win Grandpa back.

'Now then, Grandpa,' Dad said, pulling up a chair. He patted Grandpa's bandaged hands. 'The bird has gone. It's safe to come home again.'

'I like it here,' Grandpa said, snatching back his hands as if he expected Dad to kidnap him. 'I don't want to.'

'Don't want to?' Dad said.

'I get lonely,' Grandpa said, who'd never complained of being lonely before.

Dad looked surprised. Not only surprised, caught on the raw. 'Lonely?' he said. '*Lonely*? Why, you don't know the meaning of the word in that cosy little world you inhabit, inside your head!'

No sooner had he said it, than he regretted it. You could just tell.

'Maybe I do, maybe I don't,' Grandpa said quietly. 'But I know a thing or two about what it's done to you.'

'Done to me?' Dad said, and there was some-

thing in the way he said it. I knew – just knew –
that their conversation had taken a turn we would
all regret.

'I know what you're up to,' Grandpa said.
'You're going to marry her, aren't you?'

There was an electric silence. Grandpa's words
ricochetted across the room. Come on Dad, I
thought. Tell poor old Grandpa that he's REALLY
got it wrong this time.

'Of course I'm not,' Dad said obligingly. But he
blushed and wouldn't look at us.

11

The blushing stage didn't last long. I went back to school, and it wasn't even a year since my mum had died and Grandpa was right. It all happened so fast. One day we were an ordinary family, and the next day my dad was getting married. Married! To our paying guest! I was mortified. I would have given anything for people not to have known what a faithless betrayer my dad had turned into. However overworked, remote and angry he'd been, I had always thought of him as good at heart. I had always trusted him.

I couldn't understand how he had changed so much.

He tried to talk to me, of course. They both did, but I wouldn't listen. I didn't even want to know when the day would be. I didn't want to know anything.

I was caught in a whirlpool, spinning out of control. I hated Dad almost more than Aunt Cat. I wondered if she realized how shallow were his feelings, and how easily he could forget. I wouldn't have wanted to marry a man like that. I'd have wanted to be loved for ever – beyond the grave and all. But she would learn – and it would serve her right!

I didn't say a thing at school, not even to Viola. I couldn't have told her if I'd wanted to. Some things are better left unsaid.

'Are you all right?' she said. She always seemed to know when something wasn't.

'I'm fine,' I said.

It was only when the wedding was upon me, that the news got out – thanks to Maple, who made sure the whole school knew. 'Bought your outfit have you, Rosemary?' she called across the dining room.

I turned bright red.

'What's she on about?' Viola said.

'Don't you know?' Maple said. 'And you're supposed to be her friend! Her dad's getting married. Isn't that right, Rosemary?'

I turned and ran away, spilling my lunch but I didn't care. Viola came chasing after me. 'It's not true?!' she said, when she caught up with me.

'It is,' I said, reluctantly.

'Not—?' she began.

'Yes,' I said. 'That's who.'

The day dawned, far too beautiful for what was destined to take place in it. I drifted down to the kitchen in a dream, telling myself that this wasn't happening. And yet it was. Aunt Cat's flowers sat in the sink, shining in the cruel sunlight. The smell of them made me cry inside. They reminded me of

Mum's funeral flowers, the kitchen full of their perfume.

Dad appeared just in time to save them from being thrown in the bin. 'What are you doing, Rosemary?' he said.

I looked at him, eyes pleading. He looked back at me. It was as if we had reached the very heart of something. As if there was nothing more important than what we did now.

'Those flowers should go back in water,' Dad said, breaking the silence.

I stuffed them in his hands, and left the room.

After breakfast, Dad helped Grandpa dress. Ever since he'd come home from Miss Vine's, the life seemed to have gone out of him. He didn't even bother with his newspaper cuttings any more. And yet this morning, I heard him protesting.

I opened the door, and went in. Dad was brandishing Grandpa's best waistcoat. Grandpa was clutching his cardigan. 'He can't go out in that,' Dad said, exasperated. 'It's falling to pieces. Just look at it.'

'Why won't you let him be?' I said, angrily. 'He's not a child, you know. It's bad enough that you're making him go!'

Dad gave in. Perhaps he didn't want a fuss on his big day. Perhaps he was worried about what else I'd do or say! At any rate, he contained his temper, and Grandpa put on the old cardigan, and it felt like a small victory. Not that it brought me any pleasure. I went upstairs and dressed, brushing my hair the way Mum used to brush hers, and staring into the mirror at the girl who looked more like her mother every day.

'It's time to go,' Dad called.

I remember making the decision to go through with it all. I could have refused, even then. But I didn't, for Grandpa's sake. Downstairs I stalked, determined to haunt Dad all day long with the memory of Mum's face superimposed on my own.

But when I came downstairs, he didn't even look at me. I was eclipsed. He stood in the hall in his brand-new wedding clothes and Miss Perrish – as she would never be again – emerged from the utility in a snow-white suit, and a hat with a little veil. I'd never noticed how beautiful she was before. Once, she'd been nothing more than a paying guest with pale eyes and sandy hair. Now her eyes shone like gold, and her hair did too. Maybe the flowers set them off. It was hard to tell what the difference was. Dad exclaimed. He couldn't help it. He feasted on the sight of her. He couldn't drag his eyes away.

'Shall we go?' she said. A little smile played round the corners of her mouth, and I noticed faint hairs which I hadn't seen before. Like a hint of velvet, clinging to her lips.

'Yes,' Dad said, mesmerized.

She took his arm, and laughed at him. Her hair hung over her shoulders in a thick mane. 'Don't just stand there, then!' she said. 'Come on!'

We drove to the Registry Office in Dad's car, past The Beck, where the Cutlers were out to wave us on our way, and down the hill to town and the Registry Office. In no time at all, Dad and Aunt

Cat emerged as man and wife, Dad looking relieved, and Aunt Cat self-satisfied. I was stunned by the quickness of it all. In and out we went without the fuss of the parties before and after us, with their hordes of guests and photographers and cream-cake brides. Over a carpet of other people's confetti we hurried, and when the Registrar said, 'Do you, George . . .' and Dad said, '*I do*,' I wanted to cry, and Grandpa took my hand as if he knew.

Afterwards, we drove to the famous Crown Inn. On the edge of the moor, it was the place where everybody went when they wanted to celebrate. Dad had booked a table by the window, overlooking their world-class view. We arrived to find it covered with flowers which matched Aunt Cat's bouquet. The sun shone on them, and I hated the sun today. Aunt Cat took off her hat and her hair shone in it like a single sheet of flame.

'Marriage has transformed you already,' Dad said, awe-struck.

She laughed. They both did. The waiter brought champagne. 'This is wonderrful,' Aunt Cat purred.

But the wonder of it didn't last long. Grandpa saw to that, and so did I – though, of course, unwittingly! It wasn't my fault that the sun was too hot for me, and the waiter had to pull down the blind so that we lost half our view. Nor was it Grandpa's fault that he began to sneeze and they had to take away the flowers, and he couldn't cut his food so Dad had to feed him like a baby, and he wet himself because he couldn't get to the toilet in time.

Aunt Cat smiled serenely through it all. I

wondered why she had taken us on. I wondered so many things. Dad wasn't special. He was dull. He wasn't even rich. So what did she see in him?

When we got home, I excused myself from eating their wedding cake. I was past caring what they thought of me. Grandpa went to change his stinking trousers, and didn't come down again. I turned on the telly. Aunt Cat took off her wedding clothes. It was becoming an ordinary Saturday. She pottered in and out, asking if I was sure I didn't want any cake, or a cup of tea. She smiled as if this was still her day, despite everything, and nobody could spoil it.

I turned the telly off again. It wasn't working like it used to do, shutting out the things I didn't want to think about. I went upstairs to Grandpa, but when I reached the landing it was full of cardboard boxes, and I forgot him. Dad's bedroom door was open. I could hear him shifting things about. I stuck my head round the door. 'What's going on?' I said.

He was emptying his wardrobe. The top of his chest-of-drawers was bare. Even the pictures had come off the wall.

'I'm moving downstairs, of course,' he said.

'You're doing what?' I said. I should have understood, but perhaps I didn't want to.

'I'm moving in with Cat,' he said stiffly, as if he'd rather not have had to spell it out.

I looked at the mattress leaning against the wall. And suddenly it sank in, as the legal formality in the Registry Office had failed to do. We no longer had a paying guest. Dad had married her. She was his wife. He held a new dressing-gown in his hands. He was taking it down, ready to sleep with her.

'Why've you got to move?' I said, blushing from what felt like head to toe. 'Why can't she sleep up here? Why's everything got to change?'

I burst into tears. I must have been a real sight, for Dad put down his dressing-gown and crossed the room to plead with me. 'I can't live the old life, any more,' he said. 'I've tried and I just can't do it. I need Cat. Give her a chance, Rosemary. I haven't only done this for me. I've done it for you, and Grandpa too. She'll be better than me at looking after you.'

I couldn't believe my ears. My dad, actually admitting that there were things he couldn't do! 'You were always good enough for me,' I said, putting my arms round him, and holding him tight.

'Is there anything that I can do?' Aunt Cat said.

She had come in behind me, and stood watching us. I pulled myself out of Dad's arms.

'Rosemary!' he said. 'Don't go! Stay and help us. . . .'

The word '*us*' was the final straw. I pushed Aunt Cat aside and hurried out of the room. Dad hadn't done all this for Grandpa and me. Who did he think he was fooling? Not me! He had done it for himself. He wanted Aunt Cat. Well, let her help him! I wasn't going to. Let them be an *us* together. See if I cared.

PART THREE

THE DEATH-BEAST

12

It was hard to believe I'd ever wanted to be one of those dragon-slayers or enchanted princesses or knights who went off to find the Holy Grail that Grandpa used to tell me about. All I wanted now were ordinary things. My old dad, my real mum. The way things used to be.

The days passed by uneventfully. We had reached a lull. Summer was upon us, day after hot day, sapping our energy away. I revised for the school exams and tried to come to terms with what had happened to me. I had to, didn't I? What else could I do?

'Are you getting used to her?' Viola said, one day after school.

Was I getting used to her? I pictured her strolling about the house the way she did these hot days, with Dad's dressing-gown thrown over her skimpy bits of clothes and freckled, sunburnt skin. There was no escaping her. Even when she left the room, her wretched perfume lingered, driving the last vestiges of Mum's presence away.

It was really sinking in that she wasn't coming home again. Not ever. I had stopped jumping when the milkman's outline showed through the glass of the front door. I had stopped hoping that I'd wake to find it had been a bad dream. For Aunt Cat was always there. She hardly ever went out these days, except to buy more plants for the house, and food for our tea. It didn't look or smell or feel like Mum's house any more.

'No, I'm not getting used to her,' I said. 'I hate her, and I hate Dad too. I don't know what's the matter with him. He doesn't notice anything. It's as though he's on an island, and there's nobody else on it but her!'

My voice had risen. We were in George's Take-Away, buying a bottle of cold drink, and people stared at us. Viola looked as though she wished she hadn't asked. But she had asked, and I stood by what I'd said. So, we had ironed dresses and shirts, and rooms spring-cleaned as if Aunt Cat was marking out the boundaries of her new territory. So, we sat down at night to her steaks and chops and stews. . . .

'I dreamt the strangest thing, last night,' Viola began to say. But if she wanted to change the subject, I wasn't listening. I was thinking about my fading Mum, whose photograph I took out from beneath my pillow every night, discarding the glass so that I could stroke Mum's image, skin against the nearest I could get to skin.

'What are you doing?' Aunt Cat had said one night, standing in the doorway with her cup of bedtime milk.

I slid the photograph out of sight. Her voice was smooth and kind, but I knew that there was more to her than that. There was something deep, which she couldn't hide for all her friendly ways. She frightened me.

Grandpa was frightened too – I realize that now. Like the memory of Mum, he seemed to be fading away. You never heard him about the house. Night ramblings were a thing of the past.

It dimly worried me. But summer was upon us, day after day, sapping our energy away, and I couldn't, somehow, bring myself to trace the worry to its proper source. . . .

There had, of course, to be an end to the peaceful lull. It happened this way. We had reached highest, hottest summer, and the school exams had begun. Grandpa had wished me well when I went out, and I'd been delighted that he understood what was going on. 'Take care of yourself!' I called cheerfully.

But when I came home, instead of sheltering from the hot sun in the cool of his room, as he usually did, he was sweltering in the garden.

'Why are you out here?' I said.

His face shone with beads of sweat. 'She's doing out my room,' he said, carefully, as if he was having trouble breathing.

'She's doing what?' I said.

'She's moving things,' he said. 'You know, tidy-ing and cleaning and throwing the rubbish away. She says it'll be nice, when it's all done.'

I couldn't believe it. Grandpa's room was all that was left of the old days, when Grandma was alive.

Even Dad, with his fussy ways, wouldn't have interfered with it. After weeks of trying to be nice, something inside me snapped.

Grandpa knew it. He tried to calm me down – to pretend he didn't mind. But it was a waste of time. I stormed into the house and upstairs, through the dust on the landing and into his room.

Aunt Cat looked up serenely from her handiwork. The old curtains were down. The bed had been moved from beneath the window. Grandpa's desk had been put behind the door, and his newspaper cuttings were in the bin. The cushions on the leather chairs had been re-covered, and there were feathers everywhere. Grandpa's books were off his shelves and dusted and replaced in a completely different sequence to the way they'd been before.

'Doesn't it look nice?' she smiled, triumphantly. And what was it about her? I felt like a clod, a thundering fool. It didn't matter what I did, or said. Suddenly, I knew that she would always beat me.

'You should have asked Grandpa if he wanted it this way!' I said, and instead of the avenging angel I wanted to be, I sounded like a sulky child. Which, no doubt, was how she thought of me.

'I've asked your father,' she said, arms full of frilly curtains, ready to hang up. 'He agrees with me that we shouldn't let this whole, lovely house be spoiled by just one room.'

'But it's Grandpa's whole lovely house!' I protested. 'It isn't up to Dad! This is *Grandpa's room*!'

As if to prove the point, I returned the newspaper cuttings to the desk, and slammed Mr Eldis's paperweight on top of them. It wasn't much, just a gesture, but in the circumstances it was the best that I could do.

She smiled at me, unruffled. 'Will you help me hang the curtains?' she said. There was something silky in her voice. She was mocking me.

I left the room, slamming the door behind. Hating her wasn't good enough. I ground my teeth, and wanted her dead.

It must have shown. I don't know what she said to Dad, but he was furious with me when he came home. They must have heard him, right up our road.

'After all Aunt Cat's done for you,' he roared, his eyes absolutely bulging. 'Why can't you be grateful just for once, you bloody, wretched girl?'

I crawled upstairs, exhausted with it all. I should have revised for next day's chemistry exam, but I didn't have the energy. I hated chemistry anyway. I was bound to fail.

I got into bed, and reached beneath my pillow for Mum's photograph. It wasn't there. I pulled back the covers, but it wasn't further down. I stripped the whole bed. Got on my hands and knees and it wasn't under the bed, or on the windowsill, or on the bookshelf, or even under the chemistry revision pad on the bedside table . . .

I rushed down to Grandpa. 'Have you seen—?' I began. But he was fast asleep.

'What's the matter now?' Dad called impatiently, from the dining room below.

I clattered downstairs, and told him. His brief-case of work was spread over the table. He didn't even look up. 'Oh, is that all?' he said. 'It'll be around. You'll have to ask Cat in the morning. You can't now – thanks to you, she's gone off early to bed.' He reached for his pen and started writing. 'Judging from the time, shouldn't you be in bed too . . .'

Why didn't I explode? I was Dad's daughter, after all – surely I had some of the temper that he was famous for? Why did I merely creep from the room and up the stairs to bed, where I pulled the covers over my head and tried, and failed, to get a grip on myself?

Why didn't I hit him, swear at him, demand he find my photograph, right now? I don't know.

In the end, I turned on the light and picked up my chemistry revision pad. I was being ridiculous. I'd find it tomorrow – I'd make sure I did – and there was an exam in the morning . . .

But the words and diagrams and symbols danced before my eyes. All I could think about was Mum's photograph, and tomorrow wasn't good enough – I wanted it now.

I fell asleep, and when I woke at two, with the light still on and my chemistry revision pad still in front of me, the house was quiet. Only the moths made any slight noise, fluttering through my open window and blundering into my bedside lamp, brushing my face on the way, soft as velvet.

I turned off the light. Got out of bed, and went to the door and listened. Even late-working Dad had gone to bed. Everything was still, this was my chance.

Down the stairs I crept, soft as velvet myself, drawn towards Mum's photograph, as if to a beckoning light. I knew who had taken it, and where it would be. Down to the utility I crept, where Dad and Aunt Cat slept together. Together! I shuddered at the thought of seeing them like that, but what choice had I? The door was open. I braced myself and went in.

I needn't have worried about what I'd see. The blinds were drawn tight. All I could make out was the outline of Grandpa's old wardrobe, and the dark shape of the bed. I began to edge around it. The room was as stuffy as a jungle. I stumbled into one of Aunt Cat's plants and knocked it down so noisily, that Dad and Aunt Cat couldn't help but wake . . .

But Dad began to snore, and as for Aunt Cat . . .
She wasn't there.

I stared at the white pillow where her head should have been. The darkness pressed around it on every side. I could hardly breathe. Where was she? My eyes went involuntarily to that place behind the door where Pretty Polly once had eyed me from his cage. But Aunt Cat wasn't spying on me. Not there at any rate.

I crossed the room, and looked up the stairs, imagining her behind some door, watching me. I tried to tell myself it didn't matter if she was. She wasn't a thief or child-molester or ghost, she was only Aunt Cat! I forced myself to climb the stairs, head held high, but as much as I told myself that this was my home and I could walk up and down it if I wanted to, I knew it wasn't true. She had cleaned our rooms, banished every trace of Mum, even taken her photograph away. In some strange way it was her house now – and I was frightened of her.

When I reached the hall, I turned on the light. Better to face her head on, than in the dark. Taking a deep breath, I struck out across the linoleum. If I could get to the stairs, I told myself, I would be all right.

Halfway down the hall, however, I felt a draught. It was coming from the kitchen. I went in, and the back door was swinging to and fro. I stared at it. Dad locked it every night.

I almost wished I hadn't noticed. One thing was for certain, I wouldn't follow Aunt Cat outside! So what, I reasoned with myself, if she replaced her daytime expeditions with nocturnal ones? What were they to me?

I closed the door and scurried upstairs, hating myself for not being more adventurous. But there it was. I was made that way. I shut my bedroom door and got back into bed, pulling the covers right over me.

When we met at breakfast time, there was not a hint of tiredness in Aunt Cat's eyes. Which was more than could be said for mine!

'How did you sleep?' she said, looking for all

the world as if she knew I'd been awake half the night, listening out for her.

'Fine,' I said. 'And you?'

'Fabulously, all night long,' she smiled, 'like I always do.'

It was a bad start to a day which didn't improve. Both Viola and I messed up our chemistry exams. Hardly surprising, in my case – but in Viola's, who was good at everything?

'They shouldn't put me by the window,' she sighed. 'All I can think about is Brick Barns on a day like this. I never even finished!'

We parted at her gate. 'Come in with me,' she pleaded. 'I can't face revising. Come and cheer me up.'

But I was in a funny mood. Restless. 'Not today,' I said, sorry for letting her down, but I couldn't help myself.

When I got home, Miss Vine was weeding by her front gate. 'Something's wrong,' she said. 'Can't you feel it in the air? Even the earth isn't quite itself – just look at it!'

I looked at the earth clinging to the weeds in her wheelbarrow. I didn't know what she meant about '*quite itself*'. It looked like ordinary earth to me.

'Nothing's been right since they fenced off Tyger Pool,' Miss Vine said. 'I felt it that night when Frankie ran away. It was in the air then, too.' She sniffed as if she could smell something, picked another weed and threw it in the wheelbarrow.

I walked up our path, thinking of all that had happened since that faraway day. And who was I to say that she wasn't right, in her own peculiar way?

Up our steps I hurried, wondering if my photograph would be back. Never mind Miss Vine, and Viola, and Aunt Cat prowling about in the night. Never mind even the exam results. It was the only thing I really cared about.

'Is that you, Rosemary?' Aunt Cat called, as I let myself in through the front door.

I rushed upstairs, two steps at a time. The photograph wasn't back.

'Would you like some cold orange juice?' she called, but I didn't answer her. I sat on the windowsill and listened to the squeaking wheelbarrow, and the cars on the main road. When she called that tea was ready, I didn't answer again.

'We've got to talk,' Dad said. He stood in the doorway in his office trousers, shirt sleeves rolled up, holding my tea, which he put down in front of me.

I looked at the plate. Sweetcorn, thick, pink ham, baked potato. I hadn't expected him home so soon. 'Aunt Cat's taken my photograph of Mum, and I want it back,' I said. 'Talk to her, not me!'

Dad looked as if he wished he was anywhere but here, talking about anything but this, to anyone but me. 'Cat thinks you're having problems adjusting to our life together,' he said. 'She thinks the photograph is hurting you, and I agree.'

'I want it back!' I said doggedly.

'She suggests we hang onto it for a while, to give you a clean break,' he said.

Clean break! Was I hearing right? Hadn't that dreadful day last autumn been enough of a clean break? Why, when I'd gone out in the morning, Mum had waved goodbye, and when I'd been rushed back at lunchtime she was dead! There wasn't anything more unjust and wicked than a clean break. Surely Dad knew that!

'Don't you miss her too?' I managed to say.

'We have to live here and now,' he said.

'It's my photograph!' I said.

'*You have a new mother now . . .*'

He shouldn't have said it. Not like that. It was an insult against Mum's sacred memory. It was blasphemy. Inside of me, a wave of anger rose that had been building up for days and weeks. Building up all winter.

'Get out of my room!' I said. And to help him on his way, I hurled the sweetcorn, thick, pink ham and baked potato at his head.

13

I had never felt so lonely in my whole life. Never felt so afraid. It was as if every bit of anger stored inside of me was coming out – things I hadn't even known about. I couldn't stop them. Like a blitz they rained upon my head. There was nothing I could do – except hide from them.

I woke next morning, grimly aware that though the sun shone outside, the real light was far away from me. My body might get up, get dressed, eat the breakfast that was placed in front of it, but the real me had been driven into a deep, dark place where nobody could find it. Dad called 'Goodbye' as if he had forgiven me for yesterday, and Grandpa asked what exams I had today. But I left the house quickly, without answering.

Up the road I hurried, head down. I didn't want to talk to anyone. Not even Grandpa – and certainly not Maple Cutler, picking a fight with Viola!

When I reached the Old Guildhall, there they were at it, with Ridley in between. I didn't know what they were on about, but Viola grabbed me for support, and it was the wrong day to expect support from me! Maple laughed at me, and I didn't blame her. She was right. Some friend I was. She jumped on the cross-bar of Ridley's bike, having scored the final point. We watched them ride away.

'It's going to be one of those days,' Viola said, bleakly.

I knew just how she felt! 'We don't have to go to school, if we don't want to,' I said, astonished at myself, but it just came out. 'Nobody has to do things they don't want. I'm not going. I don't know about you.'

She stared at me as if I had gone mad. 'But Rose,' she said. 'The geography exam!'

I shrugged. Something had come over me. 'Take it if you want to,' I said. 'But I don't.' And I turned on my heels and strode back the way I'd come.

Down Planetree Avenue I stalked, in full view of Aunt Cat if she happened to be looking, and Grandpa and Miss Vine and anyone else who chose to see. I didn't know where I was going, but when I passed 'Habgood. Dog Patrolling. Keep Out', I tossed my school bag through the gate. So much for geography exams!

Viola caught up with me at the War Memorial, money jangling in her pocket, and her sandwich box under her arm. 'Where are we going, then?' she said. You could tell she wasn't sure about this, but she was going through with it, all the same.

I shrugged. I could have hugged her for joining me. 'I don't know,' I said. 'Where do you think?'

'We could always go home,' she said casually. And she didn't mean the Old Guildhall. She meant her precious moor, with no buses or school, or

Maple, or Dad, or poorly Grandpa, or Aunt Cat. She meant Brick Barns, didn't she?

'Sounds like a good idea to me,' I said.

Her face lit up. 'Do you really mean it?' she said.

'Why not?' I said.

'We'll have to hurry if we want to catch the morning bus,' she said. And as if it had been decided, she broke into a run.

Without a word, I followed her through Whiteley Wood. Past the empty building site we ran, and up the gouged-out track to the place where it joined the dual carriageway. It was going to be another hot day. The trees all around us were dusty and still. We had hardly arrived, when the morning bus which linked the towns around the moor, came into view.

Viola flagged it down. We boarded it.

The driver eyed us. 'Out for the day, are we?' he said, looking at our uniforms as if he knew where we were meant to be.

'We're working on a project,' Viola said, although we didn't have a stick of equipment between us.

He shook his head, and handed us our tickets. The doors closed with a quiet sigh. We sat at the back, as far as we could get from the other passengers. The bus banked and climbed and coughed its way up onto the moor. The sun climbed too. I began to bake. I couldn't breathe. I felt as if I was going to die.

'Can't you open the door!' somebody called.

Only Viola didn't seem to notice how hot it was.

She was going home. Her eyes were fixed on the window as if it were a television screen, with all the right pictures on the other side of it.

'Halfway House,' the driver called, although there was no house in sight. No sign of habitation at all. Nobody stirred. 'Halfway House!' he called again, looking down the bus at us.

Viola sprang to her feet. 'Come on, Rose!' she said, and we staggered off the bus. Pale faces fluttered behind the windows as the other passengers were driven away. I pitied them. We had escaped – but they were still prisoners.

'You can feel the moor now,' Viola said, and you could. A breeze blew up from it, mild and sweet and unexpected after hot weeks in town, where the wind never seemed to blow.

I lifted my face and bathed in it. I hadn't realized how big the moor was before, spread like a billowing tablecloth between those few towns that marked its boundaries. As far as I could see, there was nothing but sky and hills and copses of trees.

Viola drank it in, too.

'Well?' I said. 'Where do we go?'

For a moment she seemed to hesitate. But then she set off at such a terrific pace that I thought I must have imagined it. Over a low, stone wall she led me and down a sheep's path, through bracken and heather, and into a dark wood. We crossed a rushing stream, from stone to stone, and scrambled between the trees on the other side. It was as if Viola couldn't stop, couldn't even pause. She just had to get there.

I hurried after her, feeling the darkness inside

of me being driven away. I, who had thought I'd never enjoy anything again! Being sane again, being an ordinary girl, running free.

At last, we reached a cattle trough with a standing pipe and tap. All around us, green rolling hills faded into shades of blue. I turned on the tap, cupped my hands and drank greedily. But Viola couldn't wait. She scrambled over a stone wall – and disappeared from sight.

'I'm coming too!' I called, finishing my drink and climbing after her.

And beyond the wall, halfway down a grassy slope, a stone farmhouse with sagging roofs stood, surrounded by brick barns and pine trees. Viola was running towards it. Hair flying, free, full tilt. I followed her, until I reached the trees. Then I stopped, out of decency. This was her moment. Her home.

Sitting beneath a scented pine, I gathered cones. By the time she came out, I had a whole pile of them. I threw one at her, playfully. It brushed her hair, but she didn't flinch. 'Aren't you coming in?' she said.

'What's wrong?' I said.

'Nothing's wrong,' she said.

But there was. I followed her in, and the house smelt musty. Despite the hot sun outside, it was dark and cold. Plaster was falling off the walls, and wallpaper peeled where the damp came in. Twigs had fallen down the chimney. On the stairs, handfuls of roof had fallen in. Spiders had spun nests in the corners of the kitchen sink.

'I bet you had it really nice, when you lived here,' I said, as cheerfully as I could manage.

Viola turned on the tap to chase the spiders away.

'We can get it nice again,' I said.

I began picking up the rubble, where the ceiling had caved in. Eventually, she joined me, but she didn't say anything. We found a bucket and some old bits of rag, and washed and dusted until we were both filthy. The sun moved round the sky. We ate our packed lunch, sitting on the front step. I picked flowers, and watched butterflies and grasshoppers on the path.

Then Viola jumped to her feet and said, 'We shouldn't have come. I knew it would be like this. Let's get out of here.'

I took the flowers inside, and put them on the windowsills, in jam-jars. The sun had found its way in. I could imagine curtains at the windows, and polished floors. I hoped we'd come another day, despite what Viola said.

When I got outside she was off already, climbing over the stone wall at the top of the field without giving me, or the house, a backward glance. When I reached the cattle trough, she was running towards the wood. When I reached the wood, there was no sight of her.

'Viola!' I called.

There was no reply, and all the trees looked alike, and I didn't know which way to go. Nervously, I began to pick my way down towards where I hoped the stream would be. I tripped over a branch covered by long grass, and fell. A bird flew up into the sky. But still there was no sound of Viola.

I got to my feet and stumbled on, between trees, down rabbit holes, over more branches, into the stream, up the other side and down again. In the end I didn't know where I was, or where I'd been. I sat on a log and looked at the world around me, trying to stem the rising panic inside.

The wood was dark and the trees thick. I couldn't see the bright sun any more. I was surrounded by shadows. Enclosed by silence. I had the dizzying sense that I was back in the dark place again, where the day had begun. Either that or in a dream – the sort of nightmare where you run and run, pursued by something you can't see.

I rose to my feet, anxious to prove that, whatever else, I wasn't in a nightmare. This was really me, and really happening. But ahead of me, through the trees, I caught a glimmer of what couldn't be – *and yet it was. Tyger Pool!*

My head reeled. There was no mistake. I was close enough to see that the rocks and gravel had gone and it had risen into a great dark lake. In the wood. Right in front of me. I stumbled forward in disbelief. I would have turned around, but something drove me on. That is, until I hit the star-window!

I fell back from it, with a cry of pain. At first I didn't realize what it was, but then I saw its frame arching above my head, as high as the tall trees. And then I understood. Never mind Brick Barns, and the rolling moor. I was back at that strange boundary, where I had been before. At the border-post between my world and another one. It was every bit as real as the ground beneath my feet. As real as me. And yet, it was beyond me.

I touched the glass, lightly. Again, I had that sense of the window *holding* me. As if there were things I couldn't escape from – things I had to see. Beyond the glass the pool was boiling again, steam rising from it like a white cloak. I braced myself for Pretty Polly. *Something* was in the water, that much was for sure. Through the steam it was emerging, shaking itself free. I watched it come. It wore a plastic see-through mac, with a brand new suitcase in one hand and a birdcage in the other.

Not Pretty Polly after all, but Miss Perrish. Aunt Cat.

The trees around the pool shook frantically. Even the star-window started shivering. I knew that if it broke, nothing would protect me. I let out a cry. If Aunt Cat got me, I would surely die.

I woke up and a voice was calling me. A hand was shaking me. I was lying on the grass, Viola leaning over me.

'I'm sorry for making off,' she cried. 'I never thought I'd find you again! Oh, Rose, speak to me. . . .'

'Where am I?' I said. I couldn't make out what she was on about. 'What's happening?'

'I think that you were dreaming,' she said. 'It's all my fault. You must have gone round and round until you were so tired that you fell asleep. If you hadn't shouted, I never would have found you.'

It all came back to me. I pulled myself to my feet. 'I didn't have a dream,' I said, and my voice was trembling. 'I was at Tyger Pool.'

She looked at me. Really looked at me. '*At Tyger Pool?*' she said, strangely.

I struggled to explain – to myself as much as anyone. 'The pool was here,' I said, 'and the window, too. Mr Eldis's star-window. I was looking through it and. . . .'

'The pool was bubbling . . .' she said quietly. 'Your Aunt Cat came out of it, with Pretty Polly in his cage. . . . It all felt real. . . . You couldn't believe it wasn't happening.'

I stared at her for the longest time.

'I've dreamt it too,' she said, eventually. 'I tried to tell you, but you wouldn't listen. I woke up frightened in the night. It was as if I was meant to do something, but I didn't know what.'

'Oh, Viola!' I said.

She shook her head. 'These things happen all the time,' she said, trying to laugh it off. 'Dreams are funny things, the way they twist around. It'll be to do with homesickness and leaving Brick Barns. It's just a coincidence that you've dreamt it too.'

I would have laughed it off myself, if I could have done. Dreams *were* funny things. Viola was right.

But there was more to it than that. A question had been answered, which I hadn't dared pursue. I had been shown something. I just knew.

'Let's get out of here,' I said, shivering.

Suddenly we were both running. Over the

134

stream we rushed, and up through the trees on the other side – up and up until, to my relief, we were out on the sunny open hillside, running through bracken and heather and scattering sheep. Finally we climbed the wall onto the road. The good, dusty, ordinary road which led back to town with its shops and offices, and its new building site which heralded the end of Tyger Pool – and a good job too!

We lay, exhausted, waiting for the bus, not talking about what I might or mightn't have seen – or about our dreams. When the bus pulled up, Viola said, 'Let's go to the terminal. Let's not get off at Whiteley Wood.'

I couldn't have agreed more. I settled on the back seat again, eyes tightly closed. I didn't want to look at anything. I didn't want to think about anything. I pretended to sleep all the way back to town.

'You've timed it just right,' the driver said, when we reached the terminal. He was the same one as before. 'Everybody's coming out of school. You can go home, and nobody'll ever know. I've got a daughter just like you. She. . . .'

We walked away from him. The world where we could get into trouble for missing exams, seemed a million miles away. Outside the Old Guildhall, we brushed our clothes, and picked the dust out of each other's hair. The morning's thrill had disappeared. We were both subdued.

When I got home, Aunt Cat was preparing one of her meaty stews. I watched her from the kitchen door. She wore an orange T-shirt and Dad's dressing-gown, again. Her feet were bare and her toe nails needed cutting. She must have been sleeping in the sun, for her freckles had joined up and her whole skin had turned golden brown. There was a smell coming off her which even her perfume couldn't disguise – something hot and sweaty and almost animal.

I watched her sliding the stew into the oven. The heat of the kitchen didn't seem to bother her. I thought: 'You don't know who she is. You don't know where she lived before. She could have come out of Tyger Pool, with a suitcase of newly-minted clothes and a newly-minted identity. I mean, it sounds crazy, but so what? You don't really know *anything*. . . .'

She turned and smiled at me. 'What've you done today, Rosemary?' she said, and though her voice was soft, her eyes searched mine. As if she knew something. As if *she* suspected *me*.

Muttering about the mountains of revision I still had to do, I hurried from the room.

14

Next morning, Viola and I arrived at school with forged notes which somehow got us out of trouble, but not out of our geography exam, which we had to sit in the lunch hour while everybody else stretched out beneath the hot sun with their revision books.

Why are school exams always in the summer? Doesn't anybody realize how terrible it is trying to do your best work when it's so hot you can't think properly, and it hasn't rained for weeks, and the ground is so dry you can't breathe for all the dust in the air?

I struggled through the whole week. Any effort was too much. The exams rained down on me remorselessly, but I wasn't tempted to run away again. What was the point?

I tried to talk to Viola about my dream, or whatever it had been. But she seemed preoccupied. She didn't want to know. At first I thought the dream still upset her. But then I discovered it was something else. After school one day, I found her photograph of Brick Barns torn up in the class rubbish bin.

'It's not my home any more,' she said bitterly, when I produced the pieces. 'I've got a new home now. I don't belong there. I never should have gone back. Life goes on.'

Her words hit me, like a bullet from a gun. *Life goes on.* Suddenly, Dad's 'You have a new mother now,' went echoing through my head and I wanted to run away from her, but I couldn't. I felt sorry for her. She had returned to the grim and silent Viola she used to be. And the only one who understood, was me. I knew about mourning. I'd been through it too.

The first exam results came in. They were worse than either of us had expected. 'Mum won't mind. She's easy,' declared Viola, in a state of shock. 'But what will Dad say?'

I went home relieved that all my dad cared about was Aunt Cat. He would have minded once, but not any more. Nobody need know, I told myself. But I was overlooking Grandpa.

Even though he was fading away, he still offered me books for my homework, and asked how I was getting on. Even when he forgot who he was, and what point we had reached in our family history – even when he forgot if I was Rosemary or Jane – I was still his bright girl. He would still want to know how I had done, and I couldn't lie to him. I hadn't lied to Grandpa in my whole life.

So up I went, dutifully, that night after tea. He hadn't eaten with us for days, and it was worrying me. I opened his door and Aunt Cat's frilly curtains hung at the closed windows, and the wrong books sat on the wrong shelves. Grandpa lay in his new place against the wall, without a view. A pile of blankets was pulled over him, as if it were mid-winter.

'Oh, Grandpa!' I said.

I crossed the room and pulled the covers off him, and his face stared up at mine, so old, so frightened. You'd have thought death itself was uncovering him. 'Don't worry, Grandpa!' I said. 'It's only me.'

I slid behind the bed, and started pushing it back across the room. It took every ounce of my strength, but finally Grandpa could see the sky again, and the roofs and treetops. I sat by his side, stroking his forehead and smoothing back his hair. He smiled up at me. Even my exam results didn't stop him smiling. I sat until he fell asleep, and would have remained like that, so quiet was he, so companionable even in his sleep, but there were things to do.

Aunt Cat might have spring-cleaned, but she hadn't touched the room since. A scum of dust covered everything as if, having made her mark, she had lost interest. Plates of dried food sat on Grandpa's desk, with flies on them. Tea had spilled over the carpet. Rotten apples and bananas lay among Grandpa's newspapers, growing mould.

The friendly, lived-in atmosphere of Grandpa's room had been replaced by an atmosphere of neglect. I began to pick things up: Grandpa's dirty clothes which I put in the washing basket, and the cups and plates, which I stacked, my nose wrinkling. I opened the windows, to let in the fresh air.

There was something almost malevolent about the neglect.

I put Grandpa's books back on the shelves where they used to be, and I would have taken down the curtains if I could have found the old ones. But I couldn't, and it was getting dark now, and I was tired anyway.

I sat on the window seat. The moon was out. The garden looked like a jungle in its cold light – wild and shadowy, not the orderly garden it was by day. The house was quiet. Lights went out, all over town, and in our house too. My head sank. I should have gone to bed, but it was too late. I couldn't bring myself to move. I should have taken the dirty plates downstairs. My eyelids drooped. . . .

All at once, I was awake again, my head pressed against the window frame. It wasn't dusk any more. It was night, and the moon was high in the sky. I didn't know what had woken me, but my heart pounded and my hair bristled with electricity. I looked down at the garage roof, and our garden beyond it. A dark shape was moving towards the back fence. I realized what had woken me.

Aunt Cat.

Once I'd been afraid to follow her, but now I had no choice. So much had changed since then. I couldn't pull the covers over my head, any more. There were things I needed to know about. I remembered my dream, or whatever it had been. I had to go.

I hurried downstairs quietly. The back door was

swinging open. I slipped outside. The garden was empty, Aunt Cat had disappeared. I hurried to the back fence. Everything was so still. I couldn't see or hear her, but I knew where she'd gone.

I peered over the fence. I didn't want to go down the stream bed, where no moonlight penetrated between the leaves. I didn't want to go down to Whiteley Wood. And yet I did it. Over the fence I climbed, heart clanging like a funeral bell. Between roots and stones and branches I crept, and it was a good job I knew them so well. Even in the dark, I didn't fall. Every step was sure. I was pressed in on every side, but there was no turning back. I had to know what Aunt Cat did, when she went out alone.

I passed the last fence. It was as if I'd left a harbour and Whiteley Wood, in a sudden splash of moonlight, was the rough sea. Down I plunged into that sea, and there was only one way through it. The trees seemed to push me down, to jostle me towards the place where Tyger Pool had been.

At last the building site lay in front of me. I was swept down to it, catching a sea-whiff in the air of something hot, like the glowing ashes in the Rockets' stove, and yet damp like fog. Something I'd smelt before, but couldn't remember when. I squeezed through the gap in the metal fence, and Tyger Pool loomed close. I found myself whirled and eddied to its very brink.

And there, where it should have been, I faced – a void. The rocks and gravel had gone, as if they'd never been. The workmen's hut had gone, and so had the path around the pool. I stared, unbelieving, into a huge, black hole. It was as if the earth had opened up and swallowed it all.

Instinctively, I turned to run. But I found myself staring at a row of caterpillar diggers with long necks. Like prehistoric monsters, their glassy cabins glinting like eyes, their mechanical necks drooping, their jagged claw-mouths hanging empty.

They stared back at me, and I was terrified. Darkness oozed from the place where Tyger Pool had been. Darkness and the odour, which I now recognized. It was as if Frankie was in my arms again. Rotten, and musty and dead.

I opened my mouth to cry.

A hand slid over it, nice and tight. A voice whispered in my ear. 'Quiet, Rosemary!'

In a state of total fright, I bit the hand. What else could I do? In this place there only could be enemies. The hand held me tight. The voice whispered, 'Steady, it's Julia. Stop it, Rosemary!'

But what did Julia mean to me? I didn't know any Julia, who was she? I wrenched an arm free, and span round to see – *Miss Vine*.

'Thank God!' I exclaimed, taking in the sight of her in nightdress, jumper and Wellington boots. 'I thought you were Aunt Cat.'

'Of course I'm not,' she said, indignantly.

'Then what—?' I began.

'I was following her,' she said. 'At least, I was trying to! I've seen her going out at night. She's one of the things that's not quite right. She worries me.'

142

'She worries *me*,' I said – but then everything was worrying me. . . .

'Careful!' said Miss Vine.

Momentarily, I had forgotten the brink. I tottered. She pulled me back from it. 'Let's get out of here,' I gasped.

But Miss Vine had other things on her mind. 'What's that down there?' she said, peering through the darkness as if it didn't bother her. 'Look. There. Do you see?'

I didn't even try to see. For I had heard something. It came from the dark wood, starting like a gentle sigh, a quiet rustle of dead twigs and leaves, a small footfall. It was like the first breeze of a far-off thunderstorm. I began to prickle from head to toe. 'Let's get out of here,' I cried.

But Miss Vine didn't seem to notice me. It was as if she'd found a rare plant in her flower bed, full of fascination. 'Miss Vine!' I said, grabbing her arm. 'We've got to go!' She didn't even look at me. 'Julia!' I shouted. The sound was getting louder. I could hear it inside my head, like a wild beast pacing up and down, straining its boundaries, determined to get out.

And suddenly, it did get out. The wood was alive with it. 'Quick!' I cried. And certain that she'd follow – of course she would; she couldn't help but notice at long last – I let go of her arm, and ran away.

Through the fence I squeezed, and up among the trees. I found myself caught among their branches, and I struggled to get free, carried on

143

legs that ran of their own accord against a current which sought to sweep me back down.

Against all odds, I made it to the stream bed. The fences enclosed me on either side. I struggled home between them. I could hear breathing, and a heart which pounded so loudly that I couldn't believe it was my own. It surely was Miss Vine's, coming along behind. I heard a cry. She must have stumbled into a branch. It couldn't be *my* cry. I reached our fence and scrambled over it. I was in our garden. She was in hers – she just had to be. We were nearly safe. We were nearly home.

I was halfway up the lawn, when I heard the call. Through the night it came. Over the rooftops, up from the wood, over the garden fences. A call of the wilds, and more. A stormy, awful call which, in its fullness, I had never heard before. And yet I knew it.

It echoed round my head, the most piercing, rending, the bleakest of all calls. *I knew it.*

How I got indoors, I'll never know. I found myself upon the kitchen floor, leaning against the back door as if the thing might get me, even there.

Whatever Pretty Polly had been before, he had come into his own. And Aunt Cat hadn't let him go, after all. She was down there with him. Answering his call.

15

I came down late next morning, with a throbbing headache. Aunt Cat was frying her usual bacon and sausages, turning them in the pan and humming to herself as if nothing had happened last night, and I had imagined it all. I looked at Dad's dressing-gown, which she seemed to have taken over as her own, and her slippers and mane of thick hair. Each bit of her was like the page of a secret book, and I might read the book but I couldn't know what it contained. I might search the wood, night after night – even have my dreams – but what I found would always be a mystery.

Over breakfast, I tried to keep my eyes fixed on my plate. I was afraid of her discovering where I had been – of her seeing it in my face. But though I didn't want to look, I couldn't help myself.

'You look wonderful, today,' Dad said. And she did – if you liked that sort of thing. She was changing, getting brighter somehow, getting stronger. Her eyes shone. Her body seemed to glow as if it were made of gold.

Fool's gold, I thought, as Dad took her hand and stroked it.

She stared past him, out of the window at the lawn. 'Just look at it,' she said, in that lilting voice of hers. 'It's going to die.'

We all looked. The lawn had turned yellow. Bits of it were bare, bits of it were cracked. 'If only it would rain!' Dad said. He couldn't use his sprinkler. There was a hosepipe ban.

'You're turning into a lazy man!' she teased him. 'What's wrong with taking buckets up and down?'

Reluctantly, Dad dragged himself outside. I didn't know what was wrong with him. The lawn was supposed to be his pride and joy. I followed, hoping to talk to him. Flowers were opening, but it didn't feel like a new, fresh day. It was hot already. A pall of dust hung in the air.

'Have you looked at Grandpa, recently?' I said. I had taken up his breakfast, but he wouldn't eat. He wouldn't let me draw back the curtains. He wouldn't speak. 'He needs a nurse,' I said. 'He needs special care.'

Dad filled a bucket at the tap. 'Aunt Cat gives him special care,' he said. 'And anyhow, he's better than he's been for months. He doesn't wander round the house. He knows where he is. He knows who we are. He even sleeps at night.'

He hauled his bucket down the garden. I followed him, overwhelmed with helplessness. He was spinning out of reach. I could have shaken him. 'It's because he's terrified,' I said, desperately. 'Can't you see?'

'Terrified of what?' Dad said, emptying his bucket on the lawn.

I took a deep breath. 'Terrified of Aunt Cat.'

He looked up angrily. I had chosen the wrong time. Aunt Cat's presence still lingered on his skin like golden scent – you could almost smell her there. 'I don't want to hear it, Rosemary!' he said, and he straightened up and stalked away.

I watched the water sinking in. It flowed down the cracks and disappeared. Where had it gone? There was a secret world down there, which nobody ever saw.

I raised my head. Aunt Cat was pacing up and down the dining room as if something was in the air, and she couldn't settle. Dad tipped a second bucket on the lawn. Yellow clouds rolled across the sky. The sun still shone, but you couldn't see it properly.

I found another bucket, which I filled. Dad didn't say a thing, just carried on. We watered the whole lawn without speaking, up and down, up and down. When we had finished he went inside, and I returned to Grandpa.

I put his untouched breakfast plates outside the door, and drew back the curtains, whether he wanted me to or not. We were on our own, he and I. We could expect nothing from Dad. I hauled him up in the bed, and washed his face and combed his hair. Then I sat and talked to him, spreading out his scrapbooks.

'Do you remember this . . .?' I said. 'Do you remember when . . .?'

I tried most of the day, even eating lunch and tea in his room. At night, I left my door open in case he needed me. I tossed and turned, but all was quiet. I got up once, and looked out of the window. I wondered where Aunt Cat was, and Pretty Polly. Something was happening, and we were all caught up in it. I didn't know what to do. I thought of Miss Vine. I'd go round and see her tomorrow. Maybe she'd know.

I went back to bed, and slept fitfully until the bright light of Sunday morning awoke me. The house was quiet. I looked out of the window. The sky was yellow, and the lawn was dry again. What had been the point of all our watering? I stared at the sky, which seemed so close above my head, that I almost could have touched it.

All the questions that I couldn't answer whirled like a tempest about my head. Ordinary life was disappearing fast, and I didn't have the stomach for what was coming in its place.

I went down to Grandpa, and stood by his bed. He lay asleep, hardly seeming to breathe. I wave of panic swept over me. I had to help him. I had to do something. . . .

I don't know why, but suddenly I thought of Mrs Rocket who was always smiling and kind and welcoming, who always had time for me. Mrs Rocket, who had laughed through Ellie's birth and knew what life and death were all about. She'd know what to do! Why hadn't I thought of her before?

I struggled into my clothes and rushed downstairs and out of the house, convinced that I only had to reach the Old Guildhall and everything would be all right. Through the fence I hurried, and up Mr Rocket's garden to the side door. But when I got to it, I found it locked, and to my astonishment, the kitchen curtains, which were never drawn, were drawn tight!

I beat upon the door. I called. And then, among the milk bottles, I saw the note.

> HIP! HIP! HOORAY!
> NO MILK UNTIL NEXT SATURDAY!
> THE CHANCE CAME UP, AND WE NEEDED A BREAK,
> SO WE'VE GONE ON HOLIDAY!

I stared in disbelief. Friends were there for when you needed them, and the Rockets were my friends – they couldn't do this to me. Not go away before the end of term, without even telling me. It must be a joke of Ridley's. Either that, or a mistake! I called again. There was no reply. I flung myself against the door, but the Guildhall was a fortress. There was no way of getting in.

No way of getting in? Suddenly, I remembered the sliding kitchen sash. I tried it. At first it didn't budge, and I thought Mr Rocket must have mended it, like he'd mended the door. But I tried again, in an attempt born of desperation, and it crashed down.

I tore aside the curtains and clambered over a pile of draining dishes. 'Viola!' I called. I was beside myself. I didn't care if I woke them all. It didn't bother me that I was breaking in. There was only one thing on my mind. I had to prove that the stupid note had been a mistake.

The coolness of the house rose to greet me from flagstone floors and thick walls. On any other morning, I'd have been glad of it. But not today. What I wanted was a busy house – stove on, smoke billowing, curtains drawn back, sun pouring in. A house that teemed with life.

I hurried down to the living room. 'Wake up!' I called, banging on the boards above my head. 'Hey Viola. Everyone. It's me!'

My efforts were met by silence, but it made no difference. Nothing could have stopped me by this time. They were asleep, I told myself, opening the stairs' door and beginning to climb. They were up there, all of them. I needed them. They had to be.

I reached the top, and clothes lay scattered on empty beds. A forgotten suitcase stood in the middle of the floor, left behind, lonely evidence of a chaotic departure. I stared at it. The note for the milkman had been right. They had gone on holiday.

I imagined them shouting, 'Hold Ellie, somebody. . . .' 'Where are the nappies. . . ?' 'Have you got the cricket bats . . .?' 'Where's the note for the milkman . . .?' 'Look at the time. . . .'

Standing there, I could smell their baby smells, washing smells, perfume, woollen blankets, socks, the smell of their laughter, a whole potpourri of memories that filled me with despair. For now what was I to do?

The star-window shone upon my misery. I stared at it, soaring in a great arch above my head, set in its criss-cross frame. It was so beautiful, rising above time and circumstance. It didn't have to fight and struggle and worry. It only had to *be*. 'It's all right for you!' I whispered, wishing I was anything but me.

'What's all right for me?' a voice said.

I spun round, shocked. A figure stood in the shadows, where I could have sworn nobody was before. It watched me with bright blue eyes which I had seen before.

'Mr . . . Eldis?' I said uncertainly.

'Rosemary,' he said, stepping forward. 'I'm sorry. I didn't mean to frighten you.' He smiled. I saw his broken teeth and bent nose.

'What are you doing here?' I said, remembering the last time I had seen him, on a bench in Town Square. He had frightened me then, too.

'I'm looking after the house,' he said, 'while the Rockets are on holiday.'

At the thought of the Rockets on their holiday, I turned my face away. 'You're very pale,' he said. 'Is there anything I can do?'

I tried to pull myself together. The idea was laughable. He might be Mr Rocket's friend, but he was no more than a tramp, all the same. I looked at his boots, tied up with string, and his pitted hands with tattooed stars on them. Dad wouldn't let him in the house. What could *he* do?

'It's very kind of you, but I'm quite all right,' I said, and a shadow fell between us as if he could see it wasn't true. 'I ought to go, as Viola isn't here,' I said. My voice was trembling.

He came downstairs, and saw me out, walking so lightly in his big boots, that I hardly heard him.

151

'I'm sorry about breaking in,' I said, when we reached the open sash.

'No harm done,' he said, unlocking the back door.

A shock of sunlight greeted me. I rushed outside, eager to escape. He watched me from the doorway, arms folded, legs planted as if he owned the place, light shining on his stubble-hair.

I turned, and it was ridiculous of course, but it was as if I'd seen it all before. *Déjà vu* it's called. A shiver ran through me. It wasn't Town Square. But I couldn't remember what, I couldn't remember when.

He raised an arm. 'We'll meet again,' he called.

I ran until I reached the stream bed, and it was so quiet down there, so still and green, that I wanted to curl up in a small ball like a hedgehog, and hibernate. I wanted to lie among the green and never come out again. I watched a spider on its web, and a wren dislodging leaves as it flew away. I wished I was a tree. I wished I was the star-window. I wished I was anything but me.

But I was me. I climbed our fence, and trailed up the garden. Aunt Cat was hanging washing on the line. Dad was in the kitchen. Aunt Cat brought in the empty basket. There was a smell of breakfast in the air. All the usual things, that ordinary people do.

'Just going for a shave,' Dad said.

'I'm taking up a tray to Grandpa,' Aunt Cat called, nice as apple pie.

Sure enough, there was a tray ready to go up, with a boiled egg on it, and a little pot of tea, and bread and butter cut up on a plate and a saucer of jam and a little silver spoon.

I stared at the tray, as Aunt Cat whisked it away. *The usual things that ordinary people do.* I thought of Aunt Cat with her flaming hair and golden skin, and Tyger Pool, and Pretty Polly's call, and Grandpa lying neglected in his bed. Could I have imagined it all – I who'd grown up with conjurers and dragons and the Holy Grail? Could the whole thing have been born of jealousy, and there was nothing wrong with Grandpa – or Aunt Cat?

Could everything be just fine?

I looked at the place where Aunt Cat had been, apron round her waist, holding Grandpa's tray. She had looked so ordinary. What if, the other night, and in my dream . . .?

'Still no rain,' said Aunt Cat, returning with the empty tray. 'What your Grandpa needs is a good storm. It would clear the air. It would be good for us all.'

I imagined a good storm blowing through my brain, clearing out fears and fantasies alike, and hauling me back from the brink of what I had dreaded all along. That the loss of Mum was driving me *insane.* . . .

16

I had reason to regret those wasted hours, pretending everything was just fine. I must have known, deep inside, that it wasn't, but I kept it up all day. It was like a state of shock, a denial of everything that was happening. I couldn't have stopped it if I tried. Aunt Cat was nice, and Dad was my old, overworked but well-meaning Dad, and Grandpa was just a little tired from the heat, that was all.

I went to bed that night, repeating it to myself like a litany, and woke up next morning, convinced that there was nothing wrong apart from my bad attack of jealousy. How long I would have believed that, I don't know. But the postman mistakenly delivered a letter for Miss Vine, and Dad sent me round with it, on the way to school.

And that was the end of just fine.

I climbed her steps, humming a little tune. Her curtains were closed, and there was milk in her crate – not just this morning's, but Saturday's. I stared at the milk. My little tune faded. I knocked on the door. There was no reply. I stooped and looked through the letter box. Nothing stirred. I called. There was still no reply.

I posted her letter, and walked up our road beneath the plane trees. Storm flies stuck to my skin. Surely there would be thunder today! The sky was yellow again – yellow and malevolent, as if it wished us no good thing.

It was outside the Guildhall, waiting for the bus, that it came to me that I hadn't heard the squeaky wheelbarrow going up and down, all weekend. Neither had I seen Miss Vine on Sunday morning, on the way to church or coming home again. Nor had her windows been open in all this heat.

Such little things. Yet, when the bus came along, I couldn't get on. I had to lean against the Guildhall wall to steady myself.

'Are you all right?' the driver called.

'I'm just fine,' I replied. And in a funny way, I was. For the delusion I'd created for myself, was falling from my eyes. Flooding back to me, came my memory of last seeing Miss Vine.

She had been peering into the void where Tyger Pool had been. And I'd run away, convinced that she would follow me. But I didn't know that she had followed me. And I hadn't seen her since.

Leaving the bus stop, I began to walk. I would have given anything for Viola to appear beside me. But she didn't. I was on my own. Grandpa was dying, Dad was lost to me, Miss Vine had disappeared, Aunt Cat wasn't what she appeared to be. And it was up to me, alone, to do something about it all. . . .

How I got to school, I don't know. I must have walked there automatically, lost in deep thought. The first thing I knew, I was in the cloakroom, and

Maple was standing, arms folded, in front of me. 'What is it?' I said. She had obviously been talking to me.

She raised her eyes. 'What is it, indeed?!' she mimicked. 'I've only asked three times, but never mind – see if I care where the Rockets have gone, or whether Ridley bothered to tell me. I've had enough of him anyway. He has to be a freak. Him and his whole family!'

She stalked off, much to my relief. I couldn't take in any more of her. Couldn't take in anything! We had nearly reached the end of term, and there were projects that needed finishing, and jobs to be done. But all I could think about was Miss Vine. All day long, I counted the minutes until half past three, hoping against hope that I'd return to find empty bottles in the crate, and her sitting on the porch among her seedlings.

I caught the bus home, and ran from the bus stop to her house. I couldn't get there quickly enough. But when I did, even more milk was in the crate, and the curtains were still closed. I knocked on the front door, willing Miss Vine to answer, it, despite everything.

But there was no reply, and her curtained windows seemed to glare at me, as if I was to blame. And I *was* to blame. I had let a whole weekend pass by without doing anything.

Overwhelmed with guilt, I climbed down the steps and began rummaging among the shrubberies as if I expected to find a body, working my way round to the place under the steps where the dustbins were kept. Nothing was there, much to my relief. But I couldn't rest. I had wasted so much time already. I owed it to Miss Vine to search until I found her.

I put the dustbins back, and moved on. Only when I reached the side gate leading to the back garden, did I hesitate. I'd never been into Miss Vine's garden before. I had caught glimpses of it from our windows, but it might have been a million miles away. A foreign, secret, altogether private place. I imagined her rising from her flower bed, demanding, 'What are you doing here?' imperiously, and me feeling such a fool for having got it all wrong. But what a relief it would be, if I had got it wrong!

I crept down the passage, and under a trellised arch. And there was Miss Vine's garden. Lawn, flowers, vegetables, rockeries, trees. It was as if I'd stumbled upon the secret lover of Miss Vine's life. I stared at banks of every colour and shade that flowers could produce, and a lawn so green that Miss Vine must have carried hundreds of buckets up and down, to get around the hosepipe ban. No wonder she and Mum had been friends when they were young! I could imagine Mum in this garden, much more than among Dad's orderly geraniums in their lines around our lawn.

But imagining Mum wasn't what I'd come here for! I crossed the terrace with its marigolds in pots, and tried to see through the windows. But the curtains were tightly drawn, there weren't even any slits. I tried the kitchen door, but it was locked. I searched the garden, up and down – for signs of what, I couldn't bring myself to say. Miss Vine's return? Miss Vine's remains? Again there was nobody, thankfully. I climbed a tree and scanned the stream bed. Nothing down there, either.

Was I being ridiculous, I asked myself? The Rockets had gone on holiday. Couldn't Miss Vine have gone away too? She could have drawn the curtains to keep the sun off her furniture. She could have forgotten to cancel the milk. . . .

Quick as it came, the thought died. Aunt Cat began singing in the garden next door and I crouched to hide, afraid that she might see me. I heard her going back in. She would be making tea. Soon she would be wondering where I was. I would have to go. She was suspicious of me already, I could just tell. I didn't want to make things worse. And there was Grandpa to think of, too. . . .

With the sense of a job half-done, I climbed down the tree. There was one place I hadn't been, which once I'd loved but now I shuddered at the thought of going down there. I would have to do it sometime, though. *Tyger Pool.*

I made an effort at conversation over tea, and afterwards I washed the dishes, and put them away. I had to keep up my front. I had to be nice and bright. When Dad came in, I poured him a drink and asked about his day. He took his tea into the front room on a tray and, to my astonishment, plonked himself down in front of the telly. 'I can't cope with work,' he sighed, pushing away his briefcase. 'Must be the weather.'

Aunt Cat curled up beside him, among the

jungle plants which seemed to make her feel at home. The room was so stuffy. I would have given anything to get away, but I had to pretend we were a normal, happy family, and everything was all right.

Finally, Dad himself said, 'It's so muggy. I can't stand this any more. Let's go to bed and hope there's been a storm, by morning.'

I leapt forward, and turned off the telly. 'Good idea!' I said, hoping that my enthusiasm didn't give me away.

'Goodnight,' Dad said.

I went upstairs and climbed into bed, fully dressed. Below me, I could hear Aunt Cat in the bathroom. She seemed to take a long time. I was determined not to fall asleep, however long she took. Eventually, she pulled the light cord. I tip-toed to the door and saw her receding figure, moonlit on the stairs.

I waited in the doorway, making sure that she had really gone, and deciding what to do. There were two things, weren't there? One was to visit Tyger Pool. The other was to talk to Grandpa.

I needed him. I couldn't manage on my own. However weak he was, he had to fight back. I could do some things, but I couldn't do that for him.

I went downstairs, and opened his door. There he lay, like a ghost upon his bed, all skin and dry bones, just a sliver of breath coming slowly off him. I looked at his abandoned desk, piled with dusty scrapbooks and newspapers. They were memories of who he used to be – and they filled me with strength, and purpose, and anger.

'Grandpa!' I whispered, shaking him. 'Grandpa. Wake up. Listen to me!'

He turned his eyes, slowly. They were full of moon, staring through me as if he were enchanted.

'I'm going to help you, Grandpa,' I said, 'and you're going to help me!'

I hauled him up the bed, and thrust extra pillows behind his head. Then I washed his face, and brushed his little bits of fuzzy hair, just as I'd done the other day. And then I sat and *really* talked to him.

No scrapbooks, and newspapers, and stuff about school, this time. I told him what was really on my mind. I didn't miss a thing. And if he began to slip, I propped him up again. And if his lids began to close, I shook him. Never mind if his eyes were faraway. He was in there somewhere – he was breathing, so he had to be.

I told him about Miss Vine, Aunt Cat, my dreams, the star-window. I told him how Dad had changed – and how he had too. 'You should see yourselves,' I said. 'It's as if the life's being sucked out of you, and neither of you will fight it!'

In the end, I'd said it all, and yet still I talked, on and on, only pausing for the yawns which I couldn't hold back any more. I thought that if he could only hear my voice it might save him, keep death at bay, keep Aunt Cat at bay. As if by talking, I . . . could . . . rescue . . . him. . . .

I woke up, shocked, at the bottom of Grandpa's bed. Light shone through the window. I had slept all night. I had not been down to Tyger Pool. I had failed Miss Vine again – and not only Miss Vine. . . .

Fearful of what I'd find, I looked up the bed. It was empty! I let out a cry. The sheets were pulled right up, but Grandpa had gone.

I leapt off the bed, as if it were on fire, and whirled round the room. There was no sign of Grandpa anywhere. I rushed to the window, where Aunt Cat's curtains blew. I pulled them aside, and leaned out.

The yellow clouds had gone, replaced by darker ones, blown across the sky by the first wind of the whole summer. Right down our road, in every garden, outstretched branches were shaking. You could hear the clatter of their thirsty leaves as they pleaded with the clouds to drop their rain. Even Dad's stubby geraniums shook. Even our dead lawn danced impatiently.

I was about to shut the window, when something caught my eye. It was next door at Miss Vine's, moving at a stealthy human pace behind her waving greenery. I hung out of Grandpa's window to get a better view. And, as if he knew, he stepped into a small gap between the trees. A policeman in a black uniform.

At that moment, Grandpa came hobbling into the room, dressed up smartly, even wearing his best waistcoat.

'Grandpa!' I cried, rushing to him.

'I've got my work to do,' he said, brushing me aside and settling at his desk, with a light in his eyes which hadn't been there yesterday. 'Got to finish my book,' he said, moving Mr Eldis's paper-weight and rummaging beneath his cuttings. 'Where are my scissors? Where's the glue? Have you seen my pipe . . .?'

'Your pipe?' I said.

'My new pipe,' he said. 'The one I bought in town – you remember. . . .' He began opening drawers, and rifling through them. 'I know I've got some tobacco somewhere. . . .'

I rushed downstairs to find his scissors, look for the glue, make him some breakfast and a cup of tea. When I went to bring in the milk, I saw a police car out on the road. What was going on next door?

I took up Grandpa's tray. He was sucking on his pipe and blowing out clouds of smoke. I put down the tray. He didn't even look at me, but began pulling apart newspapers purposefully.

I hesitated. Should I stay with him, I asked myself? Or go straight down to Tyger Pool? Could I leave him alone with Aunt Cat? Should I go round and talk to the policeman? Tell him what I knew.

But then, what I knew was so unbelievable!

In the end, I went and washed myself, and brushed my teeth and combed through my hair as if it were a normal day. Dad went out to work. I watched him drive away. I'll go down to Tyger Pool, I decided. I owe it to Miss Vine.

But I had left it too late. I began down Planetree Avenue, sure enough, but my way was barred. The police car had moved to the bottom of our road.

162

A policeman stood by the War Memorial, with a dog. I couldn't have got past him.

It was the beginning of the end. I turned around, and ran. I must have run all day. Up hills, down hills, into the town centre, past the shops, past the bus station, past the railway station. I would have given anything to have been a train on an electric track, speeding away. I never wanted to stop. I don't know what took me home again. Grandpa probably.

It was after school, when I got back. I couldn't believe that I had been out all day. The police car had gone, but I knew it would come back again. The clouds were gathering, the wind was high. The storm wasn't going away. I knocked on the front door, and Aunt Cat let me in, dressed in black, for death. She didn't say anything about the state of me. Just smiled.

'A cup of tea?' I said, trying to sound as if I still thought everything was all right.

'I've just made it. In the front room,' she said, playing the game too.

I followed her into the front room – and there sat Mrs Cutler, among all the plants. Her eyes were bright with animation. 'Well, what a thing, Rosemary!' she said, before I could get away. 'You know they're going to start *digging* – and it's all thanks to me! I was just telling your *mother*. I knew something was wrong. I hadn't seen the light for days, and I went round and saw the milk, and I know she looks poor but her father came back with a fortune from Africa or India, or so they say. I mean, she doesn't work, does she – so there must be money somewhere. She'll have been murdered for her jewels, just you wait and. . .'

To my relief, there was a knock on the front door. I rose to answer it, but Aunt Cat was quicker than me. She was gone for what seemed a long time. Finally, she returned. She opened the door and stood there dramatically. Her skin had blanched. She looked like a stage heroine, whose lover had died.' Her eyes were wide with shock. You had to hand it to her. She did it well.

'An item of clothing has been found,' she said, in such a low voice that we could hardly hear it.

'An *item*?' Mrs Cutler said.

She shook her head. 'A dressing-gown,' she said. 'There was blood on it.'

She began to cry. I remember her golden hair, and the down around her mouth, which seemed to have grown. Mrs Cutler rushed to comfort her, muttering about not being safe in our own homes, and the police failing to combat crime. She couldn't see the triumph swimming in Aunt Cat's eyes. But I could.

'Whose dressing-gown?' I said.

Aunt Cat didn't answer me. She didn't need to – hammering inside my head, I already knew. I watched their little scene. Who was she, I asked myself, who wanted to kill, and hurt, and maim? Like a beast she had trapped her prey in a strike that none of us had expected. Grandpa. Dad. Miss Vine. Me. We were all her prey, and what chance had we? One by one, she would get us. She was a death-beast.

I struggled to my feet, instinctively. But it was

all too much for me. The light went out. The hammering overwhelmed me. The floor rose up and for the first time in my life, I fainted.

PART FOUR

THE STAR-WINDOW

17

I was in a dark place, a velvet place where everything was silent, everything was still, there was no
wind blowing outside, no trees shaking. There was
a distant, still light, but it was nothing to worry
about. I was safe. The light grew, and it was starlight. It was frost. It was Christmas Eve again, and
I was at the window of the big hall, peering in
upon the frame of the star-window, and the stage,
and the folded arms and planted legs of what I'd
thought was an angel or a ghost. . . .

'We'll meet again,' a voice said, but before I
could work out where I'd heard those words
before, an explosion of light swept over me – a
wave of real life throwing me back onto a harsh,
unwelcome shore.

I opened my eyes reluctantly. I was on my own,
laid out on the settee. Outside, the wind blew
noisily, and no matter whether my eyes were open
or shut I couldn't get back to the still place again.
Couldn't get back to the starlight and the voice
which had made me feel safe.

'She'll be all right. Poor girl. It's such a shock,'
I heard Aunt Cat say, out in the hall.

'Such a shock for you all,' Mrs Cutler said. 'Don't forget, if there's anything that I can do. . . .'

I heard the front door close. Aunt Cat walked down the hall. I didn't feel safe any more. I remembered everything.

But instead of coming in to me, she carried on into the kitchen. 'Got to get Grandpa out of here,' I thought. My head swam. This might be our only chance.

I don't know how I managed it, but I struggled to my feet. I remember clutching the mantelpiece for support, then making it to the door, then across the hall – trembling in case Aunt Cat caught me there – and slowly up the stairs. To my surprise, Aunt Cat didn't come after me. Looking back, it was as if she knew she'd got us, and could take her time.

When I reached Grandpa's room I pushed one of his leather armchairs in front of the door, and a chest of drawers. He was still at his desk. His pipe stuck out of his mouth, but I could tell he'd forgotten it was there. Forgotten everything, except the task in front of him! His face was pasty. He must have been working all day.

'Hello, Jane,' he said, looking up and seeing Mum, not me. 'Is it time for tea?'

He was my old Grandpa again, confused, but at least the Grandpa he used to be. 'Not *Jane*,' I told him tenderly. 'It's Rosemary.'

He closed his book and placed his hands on it. I began trying to tell him what had happened. Downstairs, a door banged noisily in the wind. It was the back door, slamming into the house. I heard footsteps on the path outside. I broke off, and hurried to the window.

'What is it?' Grandpa said, but I didn't answer him. Couldn't answer him.

Aunt Cat had reached the washing line. Large drops of rain were beginning to fall and perhaps it was the rain, or perhaps it would have happened anyway – but right before my eyes, she was *changing*.

It's hard to explain. Like a cocoon, the thin skin of her humanity was slipping. It was as if she couldn't contain herself any more. She threw back her head and called, and it was different to Pretty Polly's call, and yet it was the same. Reeking of trouble, full of strife and storm. I wanted to hide, but there was nowhere to go.

Above my head, the sky began to move. Up and down it shuddered, like a beating heart, up and down so low that I could hardly breathe. Closer, closer. Darker, darker. I heard the approach of a living thing, and it wasn't the sky that heaved and sighed, but the creature who filled every bit of it. The creature I didn't want to see, but it was too late. . . .

Black feathers, gold feathers, red talons, red beak. Down it came, to our garden and Aunt Cat. She reached out her arms to greet it. 'Come to me,' she called. You'd have thought she loved it more than life itself.

It was Grandpa who shut the window. Grandpa, who had stood behind me and seen it all. I was

171

paralysed. I couldn't do a thing. I heard the back door open, and knew that they were entering. I looked at the bits of furniture pushed against Grandpa's door. What chance did they stand against Pretty Polly and Aunt Cat?

It was all too much for me. I swayed on my feet, almost hoping that I would faint and return to that velvet place where I had felt safe. I remembered the starlight, the frost, the silver stage, the man. . . .

The man.

I reached out to steady myself, and my hand closed on Mr Eldis's paperweight. It felt cold to my touch, as cold as frost. I picked it up, and stars fell upon the spires and houses of the little town. Stars, not snow. Shooting stars, which gathered on the roofs of what I hadn't noticed until now was *our town*.

There are moments, aren't there, that change everything. I remembered Mr Eldis standing by the Rockets' kitchen door, sunlight transforming his stubble-hair into a silver crown. 'We'll meet again,' he had called. And suddenly I knew where I'd seen him before. *He*, not Mrs Rocket, had been my Christmas angel, my Christmas ghost! He, who had erected the star-window, which shone upon all the dark and secret things I couldn't otherwise have known.

Of course.

I felt as if I'd reached a hilltop, and the sea was on the other side which I had only smelt and sensed before, and now could see. He had given me the star-scene because he'd wanted me to know, when the time was right, that only he could help me.

'I should have realized,' I said, blushing at the memory of Mr Eldis offering his help, which I had turned down.

'What is it?' Grandpa said. But even as he spoke, we heard a door close downstairs, and something rustle in the hall.

'We don't have time,' I said. 'You've got to come with me. I'll explain later!'

I pushed open the window, feeling strong again. I knew what to do, I had somewhere to go! The garage roof looked far below us, but it was our only chance. . . .

As if he understood, Grandpa buttoned his waistcoat, and slid onto the sill. His feet were bare. 'Wait, Grandpa!' I said, but before I could stuff shoes onto them – he fell from view.

I was left clutching air. He lay on the garage roof, looking up at me, white-faced with shock, but managing a sort of grin. 'What are you waiting for?' he gasped, between breaths.

What *was* I waiting for? Something was on the stairs. I could hear it. I jumped to join him. We found ourselves side by side, overlooking the front path, which was slowly being covered by dark raindrops. It was still a long way to the ground, but we had escaped from Aunt Cat. Just about.

I glanced at Grandpa, struggling for his breath. 'This time I'll jump first,' I said. 'Then I can help you.'

But there was something in his eyes which I hadn't seen before. Something contemptuous of help. Something bursting to be unfettered. I knew he wasn't going to wait. And, sure enough, he didn't. He plunged off the roof, and was running by the time he hit the ground. Running, and I had no choice but to hurry after him. Down the path we both sped, through the gate and along the pavement. Grandpa might have been a boy again. We ran shoulder to shoulder, bound together.

I could have laughed for joy. It was the sort of magic moment, I now realize, which happens once, maybe, in a whole life. A freak flower in a winter storm – Grandpa turned into the boy he used to be, body and mind alert so that Aunt Cat would never catch him, and he would never die. . . .

It was an illusion, of course.

By the time we reached the Old Guildhall, Grandpa was collapsing, his stick legs giving under him, his breath coming out but seeming not to go back in, his face and eyes red, his head lolling.

I flung myself against the door. 'Mr Eldis! It's me, Rose! Let us in!' I cried, hammering on the door, all the time expecting Aunt Cat to come bursting after us.

'What's the matter?' a voice called, coming towards us through the kitchen.

I couldn't answer. Just kept on hammering. The door opened. I nearly fell in. 'Rose?' the voice said, astonished. 'Rose, is that you?'

It was a stupid thing to say, but the storm clouds were so heavy and in the kitchen without the electric light, I could hardly see her, either.

'Viola?' I said. 'VIOLA?'

'What is it, Rose?' she said.

I must have looked a sight. She tried to put her arm round me, but I wouldn't let her. I tore myself away. 'Get Grandpa in,' was all that I could say.

Between us, we lifted Grandpa over the threshold, and shut the door. I locked it, to Viola's astonishment.

'What's going on?' Mrs Rocket called.

We hauled Grandpa down to the living room, where she rose from lighting the fire. It felt like winter, with the flames shooting up the chimney, and the wind and rain outside. She helped Grandpa to the settee. 'Fetch a blanket,' she told Viola, 'and some pillows.'

'I'm so glad you're back,' I said. I had never been so pleased to see anyone in my whole life!

Mrs Rocket smiled. 'You know who you can thank for that,' she said, 'for forgetting the suitcase with all the baby things!'

'You said you were glad to be home!' Mr Rocket protested, coming through the doors from the big hall.

'Not a minute too soon, by the look of things,' she said, covering Grandpa with Viola's blanket. 'Now then, Rose, tell us what's been happening.'

It was a stupid thing. I wanted help, but I didn't know what to say. I wanted to tell them about Aunt Cat, but I felt my face flame red. I tried to speak, but the words wouldn't come out. It was all so outrageous – how could I expect anyone to believe me?

'I . . . it's . . . it's just. . . .'

They stared at me.

There was a thundering on the kitchen door. 'That'll be Ridley,' Mr Rocket said, rolling his eyes and trying to break the awkward silence with his laugh. 'He went round to Maple's the minute we got home!'

I knew it wasn't Ridley. Grandpa did too. Mr Rocket went to answer the door, and there was no time for explaining now. I had let my chance go. Grandpa threw aside the blanket and struggled onto his feet. Mrs Rocket started protesting. I got him by the arms and almost dragged him across the floor. Viola and Mrs Rocket watched us, astonished. And they weren't the only ones. . . .

'There you are!' Aunt Cat said, standing in the doorway, looking white-faced and distressed and the sort of loving mother that nobody in their right mind would run away from. 'I've been searching everywhere!'

She stepped into the room, and Baby Ellie, in her cot in the corner, began to cry, as if on cue. Mrs Rocket went to pick her up, and in the slight disturbance I seized my chance. We had reached the stairs' door. I opened it and pushed Grandpa up into the dark, following him and slamming the door behind us. We climbed. I slammed the door at the top, and wedged a washstand, with a heavy marble slab, beneath the handle.

'We're not coming down!' I cried. 'Make her go away!'

'Rosemary!' Aunt Cat called, her voice trembling. 'Don't be silly, dear.'

I didn't answer. I wanted to curl into a little ball and die. I was terrified of her capacity to get the

Rockets on her side, and furious with myself for not explaining when I'd had the chance.

I had been stupid. I hated myself. I looked at Grandpa, who had huddled against the star-window, as far away as he could get from the wedged door. If anything happened to him, it would be my fault.

I looked at the star-window. Star-window, indeed! Why had I called it that? No light shone through it now, to show off its special powers when they were needed. I would have laughed if it hadn't mattered so much. The window was made of old glass, and the frame was rusting. The whole thing was cracked and dirty, when you got up close enough to see. And where was Mr Eldis, who had offered to help me . . .?

There was silence down below. Not even whispering. I looked at Grandpa. His eyes glinted back at me. It was so dark outside, that I could hardly see him properly.

'Are you all right?' I whispered.

'I think she's gone,' he said.

But no sooner had he said it, than the stairs' door opened down below. We heard the boards creak as somebody began to climb. 'Go away!' I called, looking for something with which to defend myself.

'Don't be afraid,' said Viola. 'It's only me.'

'Are you alone?' I said. I couldn't trust anyone, not even her.

'I swear it,' she said.

Holding a wicker chair in front of me, I let her in.

'She's gone,' she said, switching on the light. 'Honestly. You don't need to look like that. Mum suggested that you stay until the morning, and your Aunt Cat said she'd do anything to avoid a fuss, as long as it was no trouble for us.'

Before I could say anything, Mrs Rocket came bustling in behind her, with spare sheets for our beds. I couldn't believe it. Even the sight of her made me feel secure. A wave of relief washed over me. Now I could tell them everything, and they would protect me.

I had been given a second chance.

I listened to the rain falling outside. I felt snug and safe. We made up the beds, and Mrs Rocket brought up cocoa for Grandpa, and some sandwiches, which he didn't eat. She got him into bed, in a pair of Mr Rocket's pyjamas, and pulled a screen around the bed to give him privacy. I turned away from him, savouring the sounds and smells, and imagining that he and I would stay for ever. We would never go home.

'I've got to talk to you,' I said to Mrs Rocket.

We went downstairs, and sat beside the log fire. Ridley returned. We all ate tea. I plucked up my courage and told them everything. They listened to me without interruption. Their faces were a picture of gravity.

When I had finished, Mrs Rocket took a deep breath and said, 'You've had a hard time, Rose. I think you, too, ought to be in bed.'

I protested. But it was as if she knew my deepest need. 'We'll sort it all out later, Rose,' she promised me.

I woke up in the night. There were voices talking inside my head. One of them said, 'They're keeping him in.' The other one said, 'Oh, no. The poor child. She's confused enough, already.' The first one said, 'What are we going to do?' The second one said, 'We'll tell her in the morning.' The first one said, 'Yes Jim, but what are we going to do. . . ?'

On and on they went. I couldn't take it all in, but gradually it came to me that they weren't inside my head. They came from Mr and Mrs Rocket, pacing up and down beneath me in the living room.

I struggled to understand. Somebody was being kept somewhere – but it wasn't my dad. Somebody was a poor, confused child – but she wasn't me. They were going to tell her in the morning, whoever she was – but she wasn't me, no, she wasn't me. . . .

I drifted back to sleep – the unnatural sleep of deepest fright, when it's safest not to dream, and better not to wake up.

18

Safe or not, I dreamt of black rain, black rain streaming down the star-window into a flood at the foot of my bed. I awoke, and rain still thundered over my head. It was another dark day. No sunshine. I had slept late. I had wasted time. There were things to do.

I jumped out of bed, dressed as quickly as possible, and ran downstairs into the living room, where the smell of last night's fire mingled with this morning's breakfast of coffee and toast. I heard the Rockets' voices in the kitchen, and ran up the steps to join them. They stopped talking when I came in. They turned and looked at me, and I remembered everything I'd said last night, and knew that they hadn't believed me. They hadn't been able to take it in. Even Viola, who had shared my dream.

She turned back to Ellie in her highchair, and Mrs Rocket started buttering toast again. Mr Rocket shouted at Ridley to find his school bag. He lifted a pan of eggs off the stove, saying that there was no excuse for not going in. It was the end of term. They ought to get their things.

I had forgotten that it was the last morning of term, when everybody cleared out their desks and brought home their work. Forgotten all sorts of things that would have been important once. I stared at them from a million miles away. Stared at the ordinary things that ordinary people do – the things I used to do, in a world that never changed.

Mr Rocket dumped the eggs down on the table. Ellie spat her breakfast off her spoon. Mrs Rocket said, 'The police would like to question you,' in a voice that was gentle and pitying.

I stood before her, frozen. I couldn't think. I couldn't feel. I didn't know what to do.

'They called last night,' Mr Rocket said, his voice pitying too. 'I volunteered to take you in. I've got to go into town this morning, anyway. I need to buy some paint.'

I didn't want the Rockets pitying me. I wanted Dad. I remembered that phrase from in the night. *Keeping him in.* 'What's happening?' I managed at last.

None of them would look at me properly. 'Eat your breakfast,' Mr Rocket said, 'and then we'll go. The police will explain everything.'

I tried to eat as if it were a normal day. I don't know why. I was the only one who did! Ridley sat clutching his school bag. Viola pushed her boiled egg away. Even Mrs Rocket's lips were pursed, and her face was pale.

When we were ready to go, Grandpa appeared all dressed ready to accompany us in bits of his own clothes, with a few of Ridley's and Mr Rocket's thrown in. He looked so small and shaky that the Rockets tried to make him stay. But he wouldn't listen.

The whole thing had taken on the air of a dream. He went and sat in Mr Rocket's van, and in the end there was little choice but to take him. Mr Rocket covered his legs with a blanket. Ridley, Viola and I squashed together in the back, between sacks of cement and tins of paint.

'Are you sure you're comfortable?' Mr Rocket fussed. As if being comfortable mattered at a time like this!

Grandpa didn't answer him. Just clutched the blanket, and stared straight ahead. We drove away. Mr Rocket dropped Viola and Ridley off at school. They were late. They didn't want to go, but Mr Rocket insisted. When he let them out, Viola wished me all the best, and squeezed my arm sympathetically. 'I'll clear out your desk,' she said. She and Ridley stood in the rain, waving us out of sight.

All the rest of the way, I tried to work out what I was going to say. I had told the truth to the Rockets, and they had thought that I was mad. They had pitied me. I had no reason to expect the police to see things differently.

We arrived before I came up with anything.

The rain had turned into a torrent, so Mr Rocket parked as close to the entrance as he could get. We eased Grandpa out between us, and rushed him through the double doors into a reception area, with a row of hard chairs. In one of them sat Aunt Cat.

'Well, Rosemary,' she said, rising to her feet and stretching, as if she'd been sitting there for hours. 'Here we all are, at last.'

'Any news?' Mr Rocket said, as if we were in hospital. He didn't seem to have noticed the purr of satisfaction in her voice.

She inclined her head towards him, and spoke softly. She had been here half the night, she said, and was exhausted. A policewoman came through a pair of swing doors. 'Rosemary Habgood?' she said. 'Through here please.'

She didn't tell me where she was taking me. She didn't tell me what had happened to Dad. As far as I was concerned, not knowing any better, she might have been arresting me. I was terrified. I clung to Mr Rocket, as if he was a giant tree. 'You have to go, Rose,' he said, trying to prise me free. 'Be brave. Do it for your dad.'

I thought about Dad. Not what he'd turned into, but the dad he used to be – the dad who made Mum cry with exasperation at his fussy ways, but she loved him all the same; the dad who used to want the best for me. . . .

Bracing myself, I went through the doors and down a long corridor. Rain beat on the roof, like a jungle drum. I asked the policewoman if Miss Vine had been found. I asked to see Dad, but she didn't answer me.

We entered a small room with chairs in it, and a table with a tape recorder. She shut the door, and the rain was cut out completely, as was every other sound of life. She told me to sit down, and the room had done something to her voice, flattened it somehow, and when I cleared my throat, it had done it to me.

I sat down. 'Where's my dad?' I said again, in my funny, new, dead voice.

Before she could answer, a man came in. He wore a grey suit, and his eyes were grey, with bags under them, and his hair was grey too, and untidy. He looked as if he hadn't slept all night.

'Now, Rosemary,' he said, sitting down and switching on the tape recorder. I couldn't stop staring at his huge eyes. He announced the date, his name, my name, the time. Then he said, 'Miss Julia Vine . . .' and paused, as if he was thinking. I sat in silence. He didn't even look at me. 'How old are you?' he said suddenly.

I told him.

He brought out a pen from his pocket and stared at it, as if he was surprised to find it there. 'When did your mother die?' he said.

I told him. He wrote it down. 'How long have you lived next door to Miss Vine?' he asked.

I told him about moving in when Grandma died. He swivelled his pen, but still didn't look at me. 'Where do you go to school?' he said. 'When did your father marry again? How long is it since . . .?'

Suddenly, the questions were raining down. He was writing fast now. I could hardly keep up with it all. Sweat formed on my head. It was the smallness of the room, I told myself.

I didn't want to admit that I was frightened of him. Frightened of the way he was sniffing me. Like Aunt Cat he was – a highly-tuned creature with instincts I knew nothing about. 'Do you like

184

Miss Vine?' he said suddenly, raising his head and looking me straight in the eye.

Did I like Miss Vine? What sort of question was that? 'Yes,' I said. 'Of course I do.'

'She must like you,' he said, laughing, 'to go and leave you an inheritance.'

'Inheritance?' I said. My stomach lurched.

'Yes,' he said. And he wasn't laughing now. His eyes were searching me. 'You know what I mean, of course? Your father has told you?'

I blanched. I didn't want to let Dad down, but I didn't know what he was on about.

'Miss Vine's last will and testament,' he said slowly. 'In which she leaves everything to you, with your father as trustee.'

'But I'm not her family!' I protested. I was stunned. 'I hardly know her. She wouldn't leave anything to me!'

'That's where you're wrong,' he said. And it was as if he was accusing me of something – but I didn't know what.

Anger rose in me. 'Look,' I said, blushing as if I had something to be guilty about. 'There are hardly any carpets in her house, and her clothes look like they come from the Oxfam shop. She's got an old china sink and her rooms are nearly empty. There's hardly anything to leave, and there's certainly nothing to be making a big deal about!'

Grey-eyes wrote down BIG DEAL, and underlined it, and started doodling round it. 'Does your father get angry too, sometimes?' he said, looking up and smiling at me. He changed so fast, from one thing to another. I couldn't keep up with him.

'No!' I shouted. My hands were shaking.

'I have reports,' he said, with a shrug. 'Maybe they're wrong. People do get things wrong, don't they?'

I thought of Aunt Cat, who'd been there half the night. What did he mean, *reports*? What had she said, what had she done? He nodded to the policewoman. I had almost forgotten that she was there. She produced a see-through bag from underneath the table. It contained a dressing-gown. She spread it out in front of me.

'Do you recognize this?' Grey-eyes said.

I recognized it, all right, it was Dad's new dressing-gown, the one he'd bought for his wedding. A sense of hopelessness overwhelmed me. I looked at the policeman's tired mask of a face. Even if I told him, this world-weary man wasn't going to believe me!

'I've never seen it before,' I said, determinedly.

He didn't even write it down. Just pocketed his pen, and rose to his feet. 'All right,' he sighed, as if he'd had enough of me. He picked up the dressing-gown and held the door open for me.

I followed him out. 'Goodbye,' he said, and shook my hand and hung onto it, looking deep into my eyes as if he knew there was something in there which he hadn't managed to pull out.

'When will I see my dad again?' I said, overwhelmed with fear that I'd let Dad down, and would never see him.

'Later,' he said, absent-mindedly. He let go of my hand and walked away.

The policewoman escorted me back along the corridor. She explained that a car would take us home, for now, but that we might be wanted later.

'Have you found anything,' I said, 'apart from the dressing-gown?'

She didn't answer me, just returned me to Grandpa and Aunt Cat. Mr Rocket had gone. I felt as though we had been abandoned.

'Here's your car,' the policewoman said.

Sure enough, a car appeared at the door. The policewoman helped Grandpa into it. Aunt Cat followed him out, but I hung back.

'Are you coming?' the policewoman called, holding the door open for me.

I couldn't leave Grandpa. What choice had I? Feeling small and light and helpless, I got into the car. We drove through streets I didn't recognize. It might have been another town. It might have been anywhere. All the time, I was trying to think of something that would turn the car round, make the driver take me back, make him believe the truth about what had happened to Miss Vine.

But what had happened to Miss Vine? I didn't know myself. Not really. The car pulled up. It was too dark to see the house, what with the rain falling as if every drop that had been stored up was coming down, all in one go. Aunt Cat got out, holding onto Grandpa tightly. I followed them. To my surprise, I found myself outside the Old Guildhall.

'I'm afraid we can't go home,' Aunt Cat said,

and I had the feeling that she was enjoying herself enormously, watching me, playing with me. 'Our house is being searched.'

I imagined policemen going through all our precious things, and digging up our garden in the pouring rain. Dazed, I made for the Guildhall gate. But it wasn't to be.

Mrs Cutler came running down her path as if she'd been looking out for us, a big umbrella over her head. 'Well, here you are, at last,' she said. 'You poor, poor things. You must be EXHAUSTED. Put this over you, or you'll be drowned. Come in, come in. . . .'

19

Aunt Cat smiled at me, and nobody would have thought it was anything but the friendly smile of someone who wanted to be kind, was sorry for the state of me, wanted to reassure me that everything was going to be all right.

Nobody but *me* that is, who knew that we were done for, Grandpa and I. The police car pulled away, our last hope disappearing through the rain. Mrs Cutler hurried us up her path, and we didn't have it in us to disagree. We were swept along under her umbrella. Beneath its shade Grandpa's eyes were huge and sunken and grey. You could have fallen into them.

He had given up on the here-and-now. He had had enough. He wanted to die. It was written all over him. And who was I to try and save him, any more? He'd had his last adventure, his winter flowering. Now he was fading before my eyes.

Mrs Cutler shut the front door. 'Your grandpa ought to be in bed,' she said, as if it were my fault that he was out, wilting in the rain. 'You'd better bring him this way.'

She opened a door, and together we helped

Grandpa into one of her guest bedrooms, where she laid him out on a crisp bed which smelt of antiseptic. She took off Ridley's borrowed shoes, and tried to remove his waistcoat, but he wouldn't let her. He was shivering.

'I'd better get a hot-water bottle,' she said. 'You cover him.'

I pulled a sheet over him, but he didn't look at me. He was staring past the barren room with its Teasmaid by the bed, and list of fire instructions on the door. His skin seemed stretched and thin, as if his spirit would burst forth from it any second now. I looked into his eyes. They seemed to be growing. Like black holes, they seemed to be pulling the rest of him in.

It was more than I could bear. I tried to speak to him, but he didn't answer. He didn't want me there. I could tell. Even to stroke his cheek would have been an intrusion.

I left the room and wandered down the hall. Through a half-open door, I glimpsed Aunt Cat sitting alone, head bowed, eyes closed, concentrating. Every bit of her was still, except for her hands which twisted in her lap. I stepped into the room.

'*Who are you?*'

I couldn't help but ask her, at long last.

She raised her head slowly. She didn't say anything, but her eyes burned into me, and they were as cold as ice and yet they were hot too, like a torch's beam, and I saw things in them which made my skin contract. Things which, even now, I wish I could forget. I tried to turn my head away, but I couldn't. She was drawing me in, just as she was

190

drawing in Grandpa. Sitting there so quietly, yet she was devouring us.

It was as if the game had reached its end. Pretence was gone. This was her and, tumbling towards her, fading fast, falling helplessly . . . this was me.

'Why me?' something cried inside of me, and she raised a hand to her velvet mouth. She began to laugh. The laughter grew. It seemed to fill the whole room. . . .

'I've given your grandfather a hot-water bottle,' a voice behind me said. 'And the kettle's on again. How do you take your tea? With sugar and milk?'

It was suddenly as if I had imagined it all. Tears, not fire shone out of Aunt Cat's eyes. The laughter faded to mere whimpering. 'If you don't laugh, you cry,' she said, wiping away a tear.

Mrs Cutler rushed past me with a handkerchief, full of sympathy. Aunt Cat took the handkerchief, and dabbed her eyes, looking at me over the top of it. 'You can go for now,' the look said. It was as if she was putting me aside, to play with another day.

I fled from the room and would have fled the whole house, but the way was blocked. It was not my day. Maple stood by the front door peeling off her coat, throwing down her school bags and telling Ridley to mind that he wiped his shoes.

Maple! The last person I wanted to see.

'Well, hello!' she said bearing down on me,

while Ridley stared at me as if he could see what was coming, but couldn't stop it.

I backed away from them into the kitchen. Maple came after me, shivering with anticipation. 'Well?' she said. 'Nobody's talked about anything else all day! I'm dying to know what's happening! Tell all!'

I shrivelled inside, into a tight ball. She wanted to be the first to hear the grisly details of what Dad had done to Miss Vine. Nothing but gore would do. 'Nothing's happened,' I said, hating her as never before.

'Of course it has!' she exclaimed, trying not to sound impatient. 'You can tell me – we're friends.'

I smiled at that. Even Ridley couldn't help but laugh. He said, 'Come on, Maple. Be reasonable. Look at the state of her. Let her go.'

'Go yourself!' she snapped, furious with him for sticking up for me. 'I've had enough of you, anyway. You and your family! I don't know what you're grinning for. Her father's a murderer – it's nothing to laugh about.'

His smile faded. Mine turned to ice. 'My dad's helping the police, that's all,' I said in a quiet voice. 'I don't know what you're talking about.'

Anyone else would have realized they'd gone too far. But not Maple. Tossing back her hair, she said, 'Oh, come on, Rosemary! He *did* it – it's obvious. Everybody knows he's got a nasty temper and. . . .'

She got no further. I flung myself at her, hungering for revenge. It was a good job Ridley was there, who came between us. It was his face I clawed, not hers. He dragged me off her. I tried to grab her hair and pull it, but he hauled me down the hall.

'Let's get out of here,' I heard him say, and we were through the front door before I hardly knew it, out into the rain and I never felt it, down the path and splashing through huge puddles to the Old Guildhall, and I didn't even know where we were going until we had reached the kitchen, where Viola stood, surrounded by school bags too, and towelling her wet hair.

'Rose?' she said. And then she saw Ridley's cheek. 'Ridley!' she shrieked.

She dropped the towel. Mrs Rocket came running into the room. She took one look at Ridley, and sent Viola for the cotton wool. 'It's not Rose's fault,' Ridley said, but she knew that I had done it.

I stood, sopping wet and wretched. Now they would think I was dangerous, as well as mad! I shivered in my sodden cardigan. I wanted to explain but, suddenly, what I wanted, and what the Rockets thought of me, meant nothing. For I remembered Grandpa.

I had left him lying on Mrs Cutler's bed!

'No!' I shrieked, rushing for the door.

'Rose!' cried Mrs Rocket. She tried to stop me, but I tore open the door. I couldn't leave Grandpa in that house. I had to go to him.

And yet I couldn't go to him.

It was as though the heavens had conspired against me. I'd not seen the like of it before, nor have I since. No longer merely rain, a waterfall tumbled from the sky. I could no more have walked through it, than live beneath the sea or aspire to fly.

I stared out at it. All I could do was weep. I couldn't see the ground for flood water. It was everywhere. Mrs Rocket slammed the door, and started stuffing towels, bin liners, old bits of rag, anything that she could find under it, to keep the water at bay. She was shocked, you could tell.

'When it's eased,' she said, trying to sound steady, but her voice shook, 'I'll go round for you. In the meantime, Rose, you ought to get out of those wet clothes. You're shivering. You ought to have a hot bath. . . .'

I could see, from the way she looked up at me, that she was frightened. It was as if she was realizing that something was going on at last, and it was more than she could cope with or understand. Again, I wanted to explain. I tried to speak, but suddenly I was a feather. I was so light. No words came out of me, only breath.

'Help me!' Mrs Rocket called, and Ridley and Viola rushed to her aid, and even Mr Rocket appeared from somewhere, dressed in decorator's overalls, which stank of pain. Between them, they caught me before I fell. I found myself in their arms, Mr Rocket's, Mrs Rocket's, Ridley's, Viola's. . . .

It was like the party again, when we had danced. But I had been theirs then, I had been one of them, and now I was a terrible stranger – a fainting, terrifying, mad girl in their midst.

They carried me upstairs, rain beating on the roof, above our heads. I felt as if my ability to hang on to what I called *me*, was being washed away. They laid me on Mrs Rocket's counterpane – the one she'd wrapped around herself when Ellie was born, and peeled me out of my wet clothes and said, 'We'll bring you up some hot soup, when you've had a sleep.'

The last thing I remember was Viola whispering, 'Everything will be all right,' and staring at me with huge, disbelieving eyes which were being washed away by the rain, the black rain. Black like the place where Tyger Pool had been. . . .

I closed my eyes. I wanted to sleep. But there was a voice in the rain above my head, a voice so *deep* that it couldn't be ignored. A voice in the drumming of it, that wouldn't leave me alone. . . .

I opened my eyes again. And right in front of me, close enough to touch, rain was pouring down the star-window, black tears of it streaming down the glass as if the stars themselves were weeping, and gathering at my feet.

This was no dream. It was really happening. I got out of bed, holding up the counterpane to keep it from getting wet. I put my face up to the cold glass, and behind the rain I could see soaking trees where the clutter of the hall should have been.

And between the trees, I could see Tyger Pool.

It had risen again, high enough to burst its banks, and it was black like the rain, and something was moving towards it, between the jungle-trees. Moving slowly through the monsoon-torrent, and the abandoned machinery of what had been

195

a building site. Something I recognized. It came out from among the trees, and I realized why.

It was Aunt Cat, with Grandpa at her side!

'*Grandpa!*' I yelled, beating on the glass.

But he didn't hear. I was beyond his grasp, and he was beyond mine. It made no difference, however much I thundered. He was lost to me, dressed in his fancy waistcoat, ready to die. . . .

'*No!!*' I cried.

Aunt Cat's body swung from side to side, as if the jungle were her natural habitat. You never would have thought she'd been quiet Miss Perrish with the lilting voice. Our paying guest. She was like a beast. Dad wouldn't have believed his eyes. Her hair glowed furnace-orange, and the shadows cast upon her were as dark as night.

The trees hung their heads, as if ashamed at what they were forced to see. Tyger Pool boiled like an angry pot of stew. It cracked like molten lava. It hissed forth steam.

'*No, Grandpa, no!*' I screamed.

Perhaps Grandpa heard. Briefly, he seemed to hesitate. But almost with tenderness, Aunt Cat nudged him through the fence and down those last few steps, to stand like a dainty morsel on the brink.

It was too late.

My hands slid down the glass, hope dying in my finger-tips. Before my very eyes, Grandpa was lost to me.

And yet.

It was the strangest thing. Something changed, and I didn't know what, or why, or where. But it was there, for no reason at all – hope coming through the wood towards me. Hope reborn.

At first I thought it was a light, but it wasn't light. It was a parting of the trees, as if a wind was bending them and passing through. No, not a wind, a silver voice. No, not a voice, a person. It was a person. I could see stubble-hair, and tattooed hands with stars on them, and an unshaved chin. . . .

It was Mr Eldis.

He stood as he'd done that Christmas Eve, straddling the Guildhall stage as if he owned it. '*Hurry*!' I screamed.

He had a new stage now – and on it Grandpa was sinking by Aunt Cat's side, steam whirling around them like a cloak. It shifted. I couldn't see them. I beat upon the glass. It whirled again – and there was Mr Eldis at Grandpa's side, and Aunt Cat didn't seem to realize. She stood in triumph.

For an awful moment, I thought that she had won. The steam rose to hide all three of them, and when it cleared Grandpa had gone, and so had Mr Eldis. Only Aunt Cat remained.

The rain stopped. The light of her triumph went out of her. She span around and I saw her face. She didn't know where Grandpa had gone, any more than I did. Mr Eldis had defeated her. She let out a cry.

I gathered up the counterpane, and would have fled, but when it came to it, I couldn't move. Even when the glass began to crack, right in front of me, I couldn't prise myself away. I didn't care what danger I was in. All I cared about was seeing the conclusion of the thing.

And sure enough, Pretty Polly answered Aunt Cat's cry. The pool rose to greet him as he fell out of the sky. Dark as the worst dream, he was, and wide as night his wings stretched over Aunt Cat's head. Down he came, and the two – I don't know how else to put it – the two *fused*. There were no black-and-gold feathers any more. No Aunt Cat. There was a new thing made in Tyger Pool. Or maybe it was an old thing returning.

Maybe Pretty Polly had been a part of Aunt Cat, all along. And now they were reunited. They were one. Nothing could stop them getting Grandpa, Dad, me – anything they wanted. They were what they always had been, century after century, under Tyger Pool in the caverns of a world that none of us knew anything about, though we sometimes scratched its surface, though we sometimes guessed. The underworld. The earth's core. The black star at the heart of us. Hell.

It was Viola who pulled me away, but it could have been any one of them. They were all there, even Baby Ellie in Mrs Rocket's arms. They had come running when I'd cried, and now they'd seen it. Now they knew.

I was not mad, but they had found out too late.

'Get down!' cried Mr Rocket. But the death-beast's gaze had reached us through the window, and we couldn't move.

20

The star-window lit up, as if it had been hit by a flame-thrower. It turned furnace-white, and in its light we were bleached of colour, like characters on a black-and-white television screen.

We shrank back, waiting for it to fragment. And yet it didn't. The whiteness faded. Though it had cracked from top to bottom, the window was made of sterner stuff than ordinary glass. Beyond it, we could see the wood again. We could see the pool spilling and whirling so fiercely that it made us feel as if we were spilling and whirling too.

The death-beast had gone.

We looked at each other. 'The doors are locked,' Mr Rocket said. 'Nothing can get in!'

But he had got it wrong.

Even from upstairs, we heard the kitchen door opening. Viola clung to me. Ridley's face was rigid and chalk white. It was a mask of fear. Even Baby Ellie cried. We heard something come into the living room and pad, scrape, pad across the floor to the stairs' door. I screamed. I drew back and collided with Mr Rocket, who had grabbed a chair, and was brandishing it – as if bits of woven wicker and stick-legs could protect us against what Aunt Cat had turned into! He called 'Who's there?' He sounded frightened, and small. *Mr Rocket*, frightened and small!

'Is Rosemary up there?' a voice called.

Everything stopped whirling. *I knew that voice.* We all knew it, didn't we?

'Mr Eldis?' I said. 'It's me, Rosemary.'

'Come and help me with your grandfather,' he said.

It might have been some awful trick, but I didn't wait to see. Downstairs I tumbled, flinging wide the door. And there, sure enough, was Grandpa, leaning on Mr Eldis's arm. They were soaked to the skin. Even Mr Eldis's sturdy legs were giving in. His stubble hair lay flattened on his head. He looked as if he'd had one too many nights out on the town.

I hugged them both and dragged them upstairs, crying with relief. When we reached the top everybody crowded round. Mrs Rocket plucked at Grandpa's wet clothes. Ridley laughed. Viola began questioning. She wanted to know everything. We *all* did. 'How did you . . .? Where do you . . .? Why have you . . .?'

But Mr Eldis never got the chance to answer us. The floor whirled again. It dipped so violently that we were thrown down like skittles. I fell one way, Grandpa fell the other. I tried to get to him, but the floor did it again, it pitched, and I couldn't manage it. *Pitched*! There was no other word for it. We found ourselves ducking flying furniture, and ornaments, and pictures. Every floorboard and roof-beam creaked. It was as though the Guild-hall had turned into a ship, which had hit a storm.

And what a storm! Beyond the star-window, Tyger Pool had turned into a black sea. The trees of Whiteley Wood had sunk beneath it. Even the War Memorial had gone. Through the window I could see waves running up our road. They swirled round the plane trees and up our garden paths, and laid siege to our front doors.

And above our heads, the rain started beating again. It poured down the Guildhall's walls. I could hear it. It was really happening. This was not a dream. We had passed the boundaries of reason-able possibility. This was uncharted territory. *Any-thing* could happen.

As if to prove the point, the lights went out. We were plunged into stormy darkness.

'I'll find some candles,' Mr Rocket called.

But the death-beast came for us before he had the chance.

It came with Aunt Cat's lilting voice, which I'd first heard on our doorstep, a lifetime-and-a-half ago.

'Rosemary,' it called, as if our whole world wasn't tipping and careering, and this was just another day. 'It's only me. You are there, aren't you? I've been looking for you everywhere. Is Grandpa with you? Mrs Cutler's made some tea, and it's such a nice tea. All the things he likes, and Maple's sorry. She wants you to come back, so that she can apo-logize.'

'Go away!' I cried. 'Leave us alone. I hate you. I've never hated anyone so much in my whole life.'

'Oh, Rosemary,' the voice sighed, unperturbed. 'You're tired and confused. Don't be afraid. I've come to take you home.'

Home. The word went through me like a secret weapon, which only Aunt Cat understood, who knew how much I longed for Mum.

'Leave me alone!'

I began to sob, but far from leaving me, the death-beast started climbing the stairs. Its search-lamp-eyes lit the beds and screens and clothes, all fallen down. It lit us. We couldn't hide from it.

It came to rest on Grandpa.

To my surprise, he had risen to his feet and stood there swaying, my little grandpa with his fuzz of hair and bulging chest and matchstick legs. David before Goliath. A leaf before a storm.

'You heard her. *Go away,*' he said, hands raised to protect himself from the light, which cast seering, unnatural colours across the stage.

The death-beast laughed with pleasure. 'Old man, old man!' it crooned. 'Your time has come.'

They were a mistake, those words. Grandpa lifted up his head. He said, '*If the time is right, maybe. But where my heart takes me, and not with you.*' His voice shook. I'd never heard him sound so angry, or contemptuous. His words were like a challenge, thrown down.

I didn't understand the challenge, but the death-beast did. Deep in its eyes the lights went out, and blackness burned instead. Then, across

202

the stage it came, matching anger with anger, contempt with contempt.

Grandpa didn't stand a chance. The death-beast fell on him like night devouring day. We couldn't see it, but we felt its seering heat. Round the stage they hurtled, like a fireball.

I was consumed with fear. Overwhelmed by the awful stench. It was the smell of Frankie, and Tyger Pool, and death. I screamed. Suddenly, Mr Eldis was at my side. '*Do something*!' I cried. I was beside myself. I started hitting him.

But instead of doing anything, he held me tight. There was something savage and determined in his face. 'There's nothing we can do!' he said. 'This last battle is your grandpa's. None of us can help him!'

I bit his hand, I tried to tear myself away, I didn't want to hear him. But Mr Eldis hung on, and the floor pitched, and the next thing I knew we were down like skittles again.

We rolled towards the star-window, but were overtaken by Grandpa and the death-beast. They struck it with such force that the glass shattered finally, and even the metal frame broke. The air filled with shards of what looked like stars, falling like fireworks onto the stage. Grandpa and the death-beast fell through.

I would have fallen too. The black sea rose in a huge wave, and it would have engulfed me, but Mr Eldis pulled me back. He held me tight. I stared at the wave, close enough to see things in it. Things I'd seen in Aunt Cat's eyes, when she had tried to draw me in. Hands, eyes, bellies, gabbing mouths. Creatures from another realm, faintly flickering and stretched out thin.

My heart's beat froze. Theirs was the place from which Aunt Cat had come. And now she was returning. The wave fell. I heard their welcome sigh. It signified that Grandpa had defeated her. That she had gone home.

The water ceased its seething, just like that. There was not a ripple, not a swirl. The floor beneath me rocked gently, like a mother nursing her child. I stared at where the wave had been. The creatures had gone. The death-beast had gone. Tyger Pool had gone.

All I could see was a glimmer of light.

It gradually dawned on me that I was staring into deepest night – staring at sky, not sea, staring at distant stars, not creatures of the deep. A hand touched me. I looked at the tattooed stars, and the bite mark inflicted by me. Mr Eldis smiled. He helped me to my feet.

'It's over, isn't it?' I said.

'Nearly,' he said. 'Come with me.'

He handed me through the window, as if I were one of those princesses I used to dream about on rainy days in the utility. Except that they were poor dreams, and this was so much more.

He handed me through the window, and though there was darkness on the other side, I wasn't afraid. I didn't hesitate, and neither did the others. Viola, Ridley, Mr Rocket, Mrs Rocket, Ellie. We were all there, laughing with surprise, and the wonder of stepping through the broken rim of everything we'd ever known.

I looked into Mr Eldis's eyes, and there were things in him that I'd never noticed before. Why hadn't I noticed them? What had been wrong with me? In his face were rivers that ran unfettered to a perfect sea, and woods that would never be cut down again, and towns like ours, but paved with gold.

Once I had thought he was a tramp, a scrounger, an oddball friend of funny Mr Rocket's, who made friends with everyone. When I had looked at him, all I had seen were broken teeth, and a bent nose. . . .

He laughed at me, as if it really didn't matter. 'Come on, Rose,' he said. '*It's time to fly.*'

And so we flew. Don't ask me how, for if I knew, I'd be doing it now. We just raised our arms, and soared, and coasted, and turned, and floated.

And looked down on our world.

There, the Old Guildhall, still bobbing like a ship. There, Emmanuel's church spire, and the War Memorial, and Whiteley Wood emerging from the flood. There, the school and shops and multi-storey car parks and offices. How small they were.

Over them I flew. Higher and higher, until the others had been left behind. Over the high moor, with town-lights crowding it on every side. Up and up, alone, until the stars seemed so close and bright and new. As if they never became tired, or lost their brilliance, or died.

If only Grandpa could have seen them.

I closed my eyes.

'Don't cry,' he said. And there he was shining inside my head, all the different grandpas he'd ever been, right back to the little boy who'd run shoulder to shoulder with me, to the Old Guildhall. Grandpa. Not lost in Tyger Pool, but here with me among the bright stars.

I could feel his arms around me and hear him say, 'Don't worry, Rosemary. You're going to be all right.' I could lean my head against his waistcoat, and hold him tight, feeling his buttons, and smelling his tobacco. And mixed up with his voice, I could hear another, softer voice. Within his arms I could feel her arms, and against my cheek I could feel the brush of her breath.

'*MUM*!!?' I whispered. 'MUM, IS THAT YOU?'

'*My Rose*,' the breath sighed, like a caress which touched me lightly, but I couldn't cling to it. Mum was beyond me now, and Grandpa too. If the time is right, Grandpa had said.

And the time was right for me to let them go.

Home I flew. Down, down, down until the Rockets were at my side again, and Mr Eldis, who knew where I'd been, who knew what I'd seen. Down to our town. Down to the Old Guildhall and the star-window.

'Let me help you,' Mr Eldis said.

One by one, he handed us through onto the Guildhall stage. The lights were on again. Clothes and beds were flung everywhere. I looked at the broken shards on the floor, the jagged glass sticking out of the ancient frame. I remembered it withstanding the death-beast's beam. I remembered my dreams. What was it made of, where did it come from, our star-window?

I turned to Mr Eldis. He'd know.

But Mr Eldis had gone. We never saw him again.

21

Mrs Rocket extracted a speck of something from my hair. I watched it fade in the palm of her hand, like the frost on Christmas Eve, or a slither of starlight. It was a bit of broken window. We gathered round it.

'We've done what people dream of,' she said.

There were no words for it. We couldn't even look each other in the eye, we had to look away. And all around us, the broken star-window was melting. We watched it go until only a bare stage remained, and a tangled frame in need of repair.

'Rose,' said Viola, quietly.

I turned. She wasn't looking at the stage any more, but at her parents' bed. And on it – on the very place where Ellie had been born – Grandpa was lain out like a stately monarch, his waistcoat buttoned, his baby-fuzz of hair framing him like a halo. He was smiling, but whatever brings a smile to life had gone. Grandpa was dead.

I looked at the figure who wasn't my grandpa any more. His book was closed, finally. The history of his life and times was over, with all its struggles to hold onto a failing body and weakened mind.

The Rockets clustered round me. I willed them not to speak. I knew where Grandpa had gone, but it made no difference. I'd let him go, but I still had my feelings, didn't I?

I didn't want to hear them telling me that it was for the best, even though it was. Not now, not yet. For taken in the act of smiling, my Grandpa had gone. For good.

I wanted to be alone.

It was dark outside – I didn't know what hour of the day or night – but they let me go without a murmur. I opened the kitchen door, and stumbled out. The flood had gone. The streets were washed clean. I walked past our road, up to Emmanuel's graveyard where my mother was lain. I found her stone, and sat down. What I thought about, or for how long, who can tell. All I know is that in the end, it became light. I watched the stars fading until only one was left – the morning star, watching over me.

I got up and walked home. I had forgotten the police, and Dad, and Miss Vine. Forgotten the dramas of only yesterday. It was as if time had folded up my life like a telescope, and all I could see was what lay in front of me, enlarged a thousandfold. Only when I saw our house, did I begin to remember things. Our house, and the house next door, with all its lights on. Every window burning bright.

'Miss Vine?' I muttered. 'Of course, Miss Vine!!'

I found myself running up her path. Her door

was open, and she was standing there, looking down at me. 'Rosemary . . .?' she said, as if she, too, only dimly remembered me.

'Yes, it's me.'

'Rosemary.'

Tears welled up in her eyes. I remembered the black wave and the creatures in it. 'I know where you've been,' I said. 'I know what it's like. I've seen.'

'You've seen?' She shivered.

'Let's go inside,' I said.

We went in, and shut the door.

'It was so lonely,' she said, rubbing her skin as if Tyger Pool still lingered on it. 'I've never been so lonely in my whole life.'

She went upstairs to wash the pool away. When she emerged, her wet hair shone and she wore a green dress with roses on it. Green, like our battered gardens after the storm.

We sat by the open kitchen door and smelt the scent of flowers, which had been heightened by the rain, and listened to the sound of dripping leaves and the early-morning song of the birds, so many birds, which I heard for the first time since Mum had died.

'You're too hard on yourself,' Miss Vine said, when I had finished confessing where I'd gone wrong, and the way I'd let circumstances carry me along. 'You're a good girl. Your mother would have been proud of you.'

I flushed at the thought of Mum being proud of me. Miss Vine laughed and said, 'I don't know about your father, though – unless we rescue him straight away! Poor man. Come on.'

I leapt to my feet. Where had I been all night? What had I been thinking about? Miss Vine was right. My poor dad!

'What shall we say?' I said, shuddering at the memory of Grey-eyes which came flooding back.

Miss Vine closed the back door, and locked it. 'I don't know. We'll think of something.'

Up the road we hurried, everybody watching us. It was that time of day. They were all either off to work, or on the step waving 'goodbye'. We reached the Guildhall, and burst through the kitchen door. Mr Rocket was making a pot of tea. He looked as if he'd been up all night. He looked as if nothing could surprise him any more.

'I'll get the car keys,' was all he said, when he saw Miss Vine.

I don't know what Miss Vine said to Grey-eyes. It took her long enough. Hours long enough. I sat in the car with Mr Rocket and Viola. We were restless and anxious, but none of us wanted to go in.

Finally, a small explosion of life came bursting through the double doors. Grey-eyes was there and the policewoman. Miss Vine was saying something to them. Grey-eyes looked weary, as if he went through this all the time – people disappearing and then turning up again and all his work being for nothing. But I didn't care what he felt. All I cared about was Dad, who stood between them.

His face was pasty. His hair looked as if it hadn't been brushed for days and there was stubble on his chin. He looked at me, sitting in the car, but he didn't say anything.

Grey-eyes handed him a bag with his belongings in it, including the dressing-gown.

'Let's go,' Mr Rocket said, switching on the car engine as if he wanted to get out before anyone changed their mind.

Dad got into the car, but he didn't touch me. He still didn't say anything. Miss Vine followed him. We drove home in silence. It was as if we were afraid of waking up and finding that none of this was really happening.

It was only when we pulled up outside the Old Guildhall, that it really sank in. We began to shout and yell. Dad embraced Miss Vine as if she were his long-lost love, and Mr Rocket as though he were his best mate in the world, and me. . . .

He hung onto me, in a way he'd never done before. Dimly, I was aware of Ridley and Mrs Rocket piling in, and everybody hugging everybody else – except Mrs Cutler, who was staring with goggle-eyes from the front window next door.

I leapt out of the car, and waved at her triumphantly. Then we were tumbling down the steps and through the kitchen door, and a meal was spread upon the table, and I don't know why, but it reminded me of that first time I'd seen the Rocket family. That Christmas Day.

But before we ate, there was something we had to do, Dad and I.

We went upstairs. I showed him Grandpa. We

sat on either side of him, and I told him the whole story, in the sort of detail I couldn't even have told Miss Vine. For it was Dad I loved. Dad I'd wanted to tell for so long, and yet been unable to.

'That day,' I said, 'when you were preparing for our paying guest, you *knew* something, didn't you?'

He shook his head. 'I couldn't have put it into words,' he said. 'But, yes. I was waiting, and preparing, all weekend – even if I didn't know what for! And by the time she came, there were no surprises. I welcomed her.'

I remembered his *welcome* when he'd opened the door. His welcome to trouble. His welcome to death. His white, pinched face when she had said, 'You've been expecting me.'

'Why us?' I said. 'Why of all the people she could have latched onto, did she choose you and me?'

'We'll never know,' Dad said.

There was so much we'd never know. I looked at the broken frame of the star-window. Tyger Pool *belonged*. It was of the earth, and contained a part of it. But the window? Like a border-post between our world and another one, where did it come from?

'I wonder how many times this has happened,' I said. 'The death-beast, and Mr Eldis and the star-window. . . .'

Dad shook his head. He began to cry. It would have shocked me once, but nothing could shock me any more. He covered his face with his hands, and I didn't try to stop him. I didn't even try to comfort him. For he wasn't only crying about the foolish things he'd done, or even about Grandpa.

213

He was crying for Mum, and he should have done it long ago.

I sat in silence until he had finished. Mrs Rocket called. She didn't want to intrude, she said, but if we didn't come down soon, the meal would spoil. . . .

We went down and ate the Rockets' food as if it were a wedding feast, drinking Grandpa's memory with wine. And when our plates were clear and our glasses empty, and Dad and the Rockets had gone down to the living-room, I hung behind to shed a quiet tear for myself, who had been through so much.

Within a week, we had buried Grandpa in Emmanuel's churchyard where the graves were packed against each other like the crowds in town on Saturday afternoon. The Rockets stood on one side of us, in their rainbow colours, and the thin figure of Miss Vine in her green dress with roses, stood on the other, head bowed in quiet respect.

When the funeral was over, she said, 'You must tell me if there's anything I can do,' and Dad said, 'You must be our guest for Sunday tea,' and she said, 'Then I shall bring a cake,' and Dad, instead of reproving her for the suggestion that he couldn't make one of his own, said, 'Thank you, Julia.'

After that, the world went round much as it always had done. The star-window was mended, and filled with ordinary glass. Dustbins went out and the milkman called. Days merged into weeks.

Summer blew into autumn and then winter. Aunt Cat was gone and nobody, not even Mrs Cutler, asked why. Nobody talked about the flood on the last day of school. There were no more attempts to build on Tyger Pool.

I went to school and returned again. We had come full circle. It was Christmas time. Like the Rockets' rotating tree, the world was spinning round and round. We ate Christmas lunch together, at the Old Guildhall. Miss Vine arrived with hyacinths, and we made her stay. We were a company, joined together by the things we knew.

Dad washed the dishes, as usual, and wouldn't accept help from anyone. Mrs Rocket produced her riddle, and we all laughed and Viola won. She was full of fun. Plainly she wasn't missing Brick Barns, as she had done last year. I turned the handle on the Christmas tree. The candles winked at us, like bright stars. Life went on.